I0588274

NIGHT OF THE ZANDIANS

A REVERSE HAREM ALIEN WARRIOR ROMANCE

RENEE ROSE

REBEL WEST

BURNING DESIRES

Copyright © March 2018 Night of the Zandians by Renee Rose and Rebel West

All rights reserved. This copy is intended for the original purchaser of this e-book ONLY. No part of this e-book may be reproduced, scanned, or distributed in any printed or electronic form without prior written permission from the author. Please do not participate in or encourage piracy of copyrighted materials in violation of the author's rights. Purchase only authorized editions.

Published in the United States of America

Renee Rose Romance and Rebel West

Editor: Edits by MJ

This e-book is a work of fiction. While reference might be made to actual historical events or existing locations, the names, characters, places and incidents are either the product of the author's imaginations or are used fictitiously, and any resemblance to actual persons, living or dead, business establishments, events, or locales is entirely coincidental.

This book contains descriptions of many BDSM and sexual practices, but this is a work of fiction and, as such, should not be used in any way as a guide. The author and publisher will not be responsible for any loss, harm, injury, or death resulting from use of the information contained within. In other words, don't try this at home, folks!

CONTENTS

1

Riya

The Zandians require brides.

Prince Zander—no, *King* Zander now that he's taken back his planet—stands in front of all of us, human and Zandians alike, and makes his intentions for repopulation clear.

I gaze around at the throng gathered in front of what used to be the palace. Everything seems so vast and empty under a bright sky, devoid of any cloud cover. The Zandian sun reflects off the white marble stone that makes up the rubble, nearly blinding me.

How can such a small group possibly ever rebuild this planet, dedicated as they—we— are?

The devastation in Zandia's capital is so absolute that it makes me sick to my stomach. The crumbled ruins of once-majestic buildings, now heaps of marble rubble and twisted metal, look as gruesome as any bloody wound I tended during the battle.

I shouldn't care—it's not my planet. My planet was raped and ruined a thousand years ago by the Ocretions, but Zandia's been dangled in front of us humans like Shangri-La. A place we'll be able to be free.

Supposedly.

But what Zander's saying now puts ice cold fear into me.

A shiver runs down my spine and I can't stop my gaze from flicking to the giant Zandian warrior across the plaza.

Tarren.

The one whose firm thigh I straddled when I sewed up the gash splitting the side of his face. He's standing with two other Zandians and—sweet Mother Earth—they're all looking at me.

A lock of my thick black hair blows into my face on a hot, dry wind that smells of nothing except ash. I brush it back with impatience, then wipe more dust from my strong thighs, bare beneath my short tunic. I haven't had a chance to wash or change since the battle—I've been tending the wounded non-stop. The warrior beside Tarren lets his gaze slide to my bare legs and heat crawls up my neck. I should've found a pair of leggings before this meeting.

"If you wish to receive a land and homestead grant, I suggest you form a group, find a female, and ready yourselves to petition," King Zander declares.

My stomach knots. *Find a female.*

I'm not an idiot. I know what that means for me. For the other human females of breeding age. We've just become breeders. We're probably no better off than any breeding slave in the galaxy.

My mouth goes dry and I have to will myself not to look across the plaza at the warrior again. Will he and his friends come for me? Claim me? How will it work? Do I have to be willing, or can they just carry me off?

King Zander has said we're no longer slaves, yet there's nowhere else we can go in the galaxy where our freedom will be recognized. In other words, we have no choice but to accept whatever the Zandians offer.

And it sounds to me like my only option is to become a Zandian bride.

I scrunch up my hands at my sides, not because I'm making fists to defend myself, but to stop my fingers from shaking.

I don't want to be claimed by one alien warrior, much less two or three. Or—stars forbid—more.

I barely hear the rest of the announcement, and when the gathering breaks up, I seek out Lily. She's a human mated to a Zandian and sister to the king's mate. She might know more about what I can expect.

Already the air in the plaza crackles with sexual tension, as if the king's proclamation has every warrior ready to fight to claim a female.

There are no more Zandian females—at least none who are unmated—so the females King Zander referred to are human. Former slaves, like me.

Oh hell. I tug my tunic down as if I can make it grow to cover my bare thighs.

Several Zandian warriors eye me from across the cracked plaza. I really should have changed my clothes before I came out. I suddenly realize how provocative my boots must look below bare legs.

On the training pod, we females were protected by warriors like Lundric, who has a human mate. I was able to dress for pure comfort and ignore any interest my bare skin garnered. After what I've endured at the hands of the Ocretians, I preferred to keep myself apart.

I find Lily, but she's talking with her mate. I sense warriors closing in on me from all sides.

Fuck.

Like a coward, I run.

I head straight for the makeshift medbay where I've been working all night. It's a stupid place to go, but I haven't been assigned a new room yet, and I don't know where else to hide.

As soon as I'm there, though, the memory of treating Tarren's wounds comes rushing back.

The way my core heated standing so close to him. The way he gripped my buttocks when I stitched his cheek with the needle.

I lean against the metal wall of the crashed ship which became my headquarters, to steady my breath.

I'm not interested in the male. I'm not interested in any male.

Of course, it may not matter what I'm interested in.

King Zander wants the planet repopulated.

As soon as possible.

T *arren*

"Looks like you've already picked out our mate." My cousin Jax follows my gaze to the dark-haired beauty streaking across the plaza. It's all I can do not to chase her down, toss her over my shoulder, and carry her back to our quarters right now.

Without saying it out loud, Jax and I both know we'll

apply as a team with our other cousin, Ronan. We're family and we stick together.

Jax wears a bemused expression. He glances around the desolate wasteland of rubble, so different from the planet we left as children just before the invasion. "She's a good choice. With the boots she's sexy as hell, but she looks sturdy enough for—"

He stops when my fist wraps in his tunic. "She's more than a *vecking* breeder," I growl.

Jax holds up his hands. "All right, all right. She's way more. Looks smart. She's the medic, right?"

"Riya."

She looked at me earlier and blushed, just as she had when she treated my wounds last night. When I had my hand under that short tunic cupping her tight little ass. *Veck.* I'm hard just thinking about it. "Her name is Riya." Her name sounds exotic and delicious, like she looks.

"We need to claim her," I tell Jax, and scowl. I don't even know why I'm saying this—I don't want a female. But I'm sure as *veck* not letting this one slip through my fingers, either. "Before another warrior does." My fists close at the thought of some other Zandian with Riya.

"I think she's already yours, cousin."

I want to throat-punch Jax for his characteristic light-hearted and positive outlook.

"No. You need to charm her. You and Ronan. She'll be afraid of me."

Jax eyes me, not missing that I'm holding something back. "What did you do to her?"

"What did I miss?" Ronan comes up in a hurry, panting as he jogs. "I was on guard duty onboard the palatial pod and just got relieved."

"What did you miss?" Jax rolls his eyes. "Just about the

most life-altering thing you can ever imagine. Great planet rotation to be lazy."

"Go *veck* yourself." Ronan punches him in the arm. "Tell me," he demands, more seriously this time, picking up on the tension in the courtyard.

"It appears," Jax says, his voice collected, "the three of us are going to share one mate. A human. From what the king just announced, it sounds like Zandians can apply as a team, which must include a female, to receive a homestead here."

"Hot Zandian star!" The thrill in Ronan's voice is evident. "It's about time. I've been dreaming of a nice little Zandian homestead my whole life. And a female to share? That just sweetens it all the more. This is the best news I could imagine." He throws his arms around our shoulders. He laughs out loud. "This is the best planet rotation, cousins!"

"You don't care that we all have to share one mate?" My voice comes out more forcefully than I intend. Yes, we've shared females, the three of us, in random encounters, and we all enjoyed it that way. But long-term, a mate with whom we are expected to bond and protect? It seems complex and troublesome. What if I want to kill them both every time they touch Riya?

There's no doubt in my mind now that she'll be our female. I've been dying to claim her lush little body from the moment I saw her out on the battlefield trying to drag the wounded in by herself.

She's fierce. And the way she lifted her chin when I threatened to warm her ass for leaving the safety of the downed ship was adorable. A little warrior exists behind that alluring peachy flesh of hers.

And then there's those *vecking* thighs...

Stars, if I don't get to be the one to pry them open and taste her honey first, I might throttle both my cousins.

Ronan smiles, and I scowl again. Ronan is always so... excited about things. It irritates the *veck* out of me. "I never thought I'd be lucky enough to get a mate." Ronan shrugs. "I don't mind. I share everything with you two, anyway. Why not our future?"

Easy for him to say. With his ever-present smile and jokes, Ronan has a way of making friends with any and every being in the galaxy. Naturally Ronan wouldn't mind anything.

"Which female do we get? Is it the one with the bare thighs?" Ronan leans to look in the direction of the medbay. "Is she... ours?"

I'm simultaneously relieved and pissed that Ronan's already picked the same female Jax and I agreed on. At least we won't argue, but I hate that he's been drooling over her. But it is interesting that all three of us have zeroed in on her. What does it mean? Probably nothing, other than we share the same taste in women.

"We don't know yet," I snap. "We don't know how the females will be distributed. I assume we have to make her willing, but who knows? They may use Daneth's gene matching technology like they did when they bought the king's mate."

All three of us bare our teeth at the thought of not getting to make this choice on our own.

"She smells... good." Ronan smiles.

"When have you smelled her?" I growl, jealousy flooding my veins.

"Calm down, cousin." Ronan elbows me. "I've never seen you act so possessive before. Don't worry, I've not mated her in secret. I happened to pass her just now and I noticed her scent."

I grunt, ignoring the relief that courses through me. Not that it matters. If I have to share a female, I'll have to accept the fact that she is all of ours.

"Her name is Riya," I force myself to say. "And I think you two should go and talk to her."

Ronan shoots a quizzical glance at Jax.

"Something happened between them," Jax fills in, although I've told him nothing yet.

"She's the one who stitched my wound," I say, as if that explains things, touching the jagged line that crosses my cheek from neck to eye.

How will our future mate feel about the ugly scar it will leave? It must make me appear hideous. The king's infant son burst into tears this morning when he saw it.

"And?" Jax prompts.

My cock starts to swell at the memory of her sweet human scent, her breasts dancing in front of my mouth as her slender fingers moved deftly with the primitive needle and thread. I wanted her then, and still do, now. "I may have... touched her inappropriately."

Ronan barks out a laugh and Jax rolls his eyes. "What the *veck* does that mean?" Jax demands.

I stare in the direction of the medbay, my feet demanding I march down there right now and carry her back to our shared chamber so we can start the process of claiming her. All *vecking* night.

"She was standing so *vecking* close—straddling my leg. When she stuck me with the needle I grabbed a handful of her ass." *Then she rubbed her hot little pussy on my thigh.* I don't share that part with them. I'd rather keep the memory to myself for now.

"Over the tunic, right?" Jax asks doubtfully, like he's trying to make this right in his mind so we can get past it.

I shake my head.

"*Vecking* excrement, Tarren! What in the stars were you thinking?"

I shrug. "I was thinking about her juicy ass. I'd already threatened to warm it for her if she left the shelter again. If you'd seen the way she blushed, you would've been fixated on that particularly glorious part of her anatomy too."

Jax's lips tug up. "I'm sure I would've been."

"So what'd she do?" Ronan asks.

My own lips lift. "*She* apologized to *me*."

Jax groans and adjusts his cock.

"And then I let her rub her little clitty all over my thigh while she stitched me up."

"Oh please," Ronan laughs, giving me a shove.

I grin back. I'm not about to tell them that it's actually true. It's too impossible to believe.

"So let's go claim her," Jax says, heading for the medbay.

Ronan follows without question.

I stare for a moment, but then I jog after them. I know that look in Jax's eye. He's the thinker in our group and when he's made a decision, it's usually a good one.

R*iya*

There's really nothing to do in the medbay. All the injured have been moved out to one of the pop-up domes the warriors set up this morning. It seems King

Zander came to Zandia well-prepared for post-battle occupation of his planet.

I walk around the empty space, spraying sterilization mist on surfaces.

I'm hiding.

If I'm honest with myself, I'll admit that's what I'm doing. I'm afraid to go anywhere near a male Zandian right now because as far as I can tell, King Zander just declared it open season on human females.

I stop and stare at the cot where the giant warrior, Tarren, sat. I don't usually think about males, but this one has dominated my thoughts from our first interaction.

He's all height and muscles, and stars, the way they ripple as he moves. He ran out into the laser fire and dragged the injured in for me to treat all planet rotation. Scolded me when I went out myself.

I will bring them in. Leave again and I'll warm your ass.

A strange tingling had flushed through my body at the threat.

I hear a step at the door, and I know immediately it's him.

I turn, my lungs jamming up in my throat.

He's not alone. With him stands two other warriors. There might be a resemblance, but I'm not sure. Zandians all look the same to me.

He clears his throat. "Riya."

I try to swallow and fail. "Tarren."

One of the warriors beside him steps forward, lifting his fist at a ninety-degree angle in the traditional Zandian greeting. "I am Jax, and this is my cousin Ronan." He indicates the younger warrior on Tarren's other side. "We are all three cousins," he amends. "But you've already met Tarren."

I take a step back but I'm already at the wall. "You're here for me." It comes out as a statement, not a question.

The males don't advance, which I appreciate.

Jax tilts his head. "Does that frighten you, Riya?" There's something both soft and threatening in his voice. Not scary, though. More like thrilling. A dark promise that these males *can* be threatening, even if they're not showing me the whip yet.

I curse the tears that spear my eyes. "I-I don't want to be claimed."

Tarren gives a soft expletive in Zandian, his look turning deadly. "You've been forced." It's not a question.

I can scarcely breathe but the question relieves me. I bob my head in the affirmative.

"By some being here?" Tarren barely keeps the question below a roar.

I'm trembling, but I'm not afraid. Not of him, anyway. Just of my past. And of the future Zander just outlined. I shake my head.

Not here. It was Ocretion slave masters on the agrifarm. More times than I can count. They tortured me so many times with the shock sticks that I'm forever infertile now.

And I don't know what will happen if King Zander finds out I'm useless as a breeder. Or when these males find out.

Tarren's hands open and close in fists like he wants to make my past tormentors pay.

"You're safe with us, Riya," Jax says. He's as good-looking as Tarren is big. His eyes hold a calculating intelligence and his voice carries such assurance it's hard for me not to believe him. "Better to be claimed by us, males you can trust, than by another group."

My brows shoot to my forehead and a shocked laugh tumbles from my lips. "What makes you think I trust you?"

His lips curl with a smile that probably makes most females fall to their knees and worship him. If they had any females around here, that is. "You trust Tarren. And Tarren trusts us. So by extension, we all trust each other."

This time I actually do laugh and all three of them move forward like it was an invitation. "That's the most ridiculous —" I sputter but stop when they are just inches from me. So close I can feel the heat from their powerful chests warming me.

Tarren puts a finger under my chin and lifts until I meet his brown-purple eyes. "No being will hurt you again," he promises.

And just like that, I believe him. Because who would argue with a seven foot tall horned giant of a male? I've seen the male in action. He's a fearsome warrior.

Ronan picks up my hand and rubs his thumb over the pulse at my wrist. "You definitely want to be claimed by us, Riya," he says.

I want to laugh again, but I can't. The thrum between my legs is becoming too insistent. The tightening of my nipples too distracting.

As one, the three males inhale, nostrils flaring.

"She's ripe for us," Ronan observes.

I squeeze my inner thighs. "N-no I'm not."

Tarren wraps a meaty hand around my nape, stroking it. "It's all right to be aroused, Riya," he murmurs. "We're your mates."

I give a shove to the closest chest, which belongs to Jax, but the males don't fall back. They don't fall back, nor do they advance. Three pairs of eyes watch me intently.

"Y-you're not my mates."

Not yet.

Already my body seems to know it's an inevitability. Moisture gathers between my legs.

"Do you prefer another warrior?" Jax asks smoothly, like he already knows the answer will be no.

I shake my head.

He brings the pad of his thumb to the crease between my brows and rubs it away. "Then you're ours." He leans forward and kisses the place he's just rubbed. "Don't fight it. We'll take good care of you, Riya, I promise."

My mind tumbles forward and I remember the way my two human friends Lily and Cambry are treated by their Zandian mates. Like princesses.

There's a great deal of dominance, no doubt about that. The Zandians are a fierce, protective species. But my friends are quite happy with their mates.

Of course, they each only have *one* mate. And apparently, I'm getting *three*.

And I never signed up for any relationship.

And there's the problem of my infertility. But I'm loathe to confess it. Because I'm not sure what happens to human females who *aren't* claimed for breeding. What use will King Zander have for us?

"Riya?" Lily calls through the doorway and all four of us spring apart. "Oh." My human friend takes in the scene, seeming to understand immediately what's going on. She clears her throat. "Ah, Dr. Daneth said he could use our help in the new clinic now."

"Coming." I bolt for the door, relieved when the warriors let me pass. Never in my life have I been more relieved at an interruption.

No, that's a lie.

One small part of me is disappointed. What would've

happened if I'd let those three warriors continue their over-the-top persuasion?

A shiver runs through my body as I jog across the marble toward the new dome. It doesn't matter, because I can't mate them.

As soon as they see my paperwork, they'll know I'm not able to breed, and therefore, not eligible for the Zandian repopulation project.

And damn, why is that idea so devastating?

2

Jax

"Did you hear me?" Ronan's voice is eager, as always.

"No," I snap. Sweat drips down my brow. I *might* be more irritable than usual from the incredible case of blue balls Riya left us all with. That, and the fact that we didn't lock her into place as our mate. But instead, I give the excuse, "I'm busy fighting this *vecking* beam into place."

The three of us are assisting the engineering crew—human males and Zandians—with the DomePod builds. I can't deny the satisfaction I get every time I maneuver the beam into place and hear the soft snick as the metal mates perfectly with the linking piece.

Mates. Mating. Even thinking the word has my heart tripping with anticipation for our female... if we get her. No, *when* we get her.

I saw the way she responded to us in that medbay. Her attraction to Tarren is undeniable, and Ronan seemed to put her at ease. I don't know what the *veck* I bring to the mating, except my sheer determination to make it all work.

I wipe my forearm across my forehead. Even my horns are full of sweat. It's incredible to be able to work outside under the Zandian sun, or what our species calls the *one true Zandian star*. After spending most of our lives cooped up on a pod docked above Ocretian airspace, being outdoors on Zandian soil makes me feel truly alive.

"What is it?" I respond to Ronan.

"I merely asked if you are eager to bed our mate." Ronan grins at me and flicks his brows.

I roll my eyes. Of course I've been thinking about getting those creamy thighs open every moment since we parted from our future mate.

Tarren makes a low growling sound.

I have to say, I've never seen him so territorial before. Sharing Riya may be sticky. But I'm not *vecking* giving up until we figure it out.

"I know I can't *vecking* wait." Ronan grips his cock and squeezes it in his pants. In his other hand, he's holding a shimmery silver bolt that will be used to attach part of the dome roof here at the southernmost section. "She's the most beautiful human on the planet. I have a good feeling about mating her."

"You have a good feeling about everything," Tarren grumbles. "Including your own eliminations."

I laugh, and Ronan puts down his bolt, somewhat carelessly—I hear it zing onto a rock—and leaps onto Tarren, roaring with delight.

They tussle for a minute until Tarren pins him, both of them panting, and then we all start laughing. Tarren lets Ronan up and gives him a hand to pull him back to his feet.

"I'm uncertain." It's an unusual admission from Tarren.

He rarely shares his emotions, even with us. He rubs his forehead, brows down low. "It will be something new for all of us. And we don't even know if she'll mate us. Or if Zander will even allow us to pick our own mates. I heard from Jaso that they'll be assigning females based on DNA testing. Matching them to the best Zandian gene donors for repopulation. So it is not certain we will be granted her as our female. Perhaps some other team requests her as well." Tarren's jaw clenches and I hoist a beam with far more effort than necessary, sending it careening toward Ronan's head.

Ronan ducks and curses.

I rub my jaw, mind racing over the possibilities. All of that sounds like a bunch of excrement being thrown around by males who really have no clue. I could go and ask my superior, Master Seke for more information. Or should we wait for King Zander's next announcement on how this will go?

No.

No *vecking* way.

I'm not going to wait for permission to mate or until they give away all the best females. And it's not about the best females—it's about Riya. I'm not going to let her slip through our fingers. She's perfect for us. There's chemistry. Attraction. We all felt it back there.

"We'll have to mate her before that happens, then." I declare.

"I want to mate her first." Ronan says, as if it will make it so.

I give him a look. "We will have to discuss it."

"Maybe we should let her choose," Tarren suggests, although the grumble in his voice makes it sound like he hates the idea.

"Choose what? Whether to mate us or which one claims her first?"

"Which one claims her," Tarren says.

Oh for *veck's* sake. Are we seriously arguing over who gets to dip his cock in her first? We need to get her pierced and firmly bound to us first. "We will go in order of age," I say with the same calm, decisive tone I employ every time the two of them butt heads. "As Tarren is the eldest, he will be first. Then me, then you, Ronan." I'm honestly not sure how this will work, but it seems like we need a plan.

Ronan rolls his eyes. "No, cousin. We will take her together." He says it simply, as if it were an accepted fact.

I nod. The idea is just as appealing to me or more so than taking her alone.

"But we will make her first time with us so incredible that she will beg for us, over and over." Ronan is all confidence. "Like the little pet we *vecked* at Prium's Sex Emporium. Remember how she liked having three Zandians at one time?"

My lips tug at the memory. *Veck*, that was incredible. Having three cocks at once made the little pet so insane with need that she more than satisfied all of us, over and over.

"We don't know if humans react the same way," I caution Ronan, although I have to turn away, so my arousal isn't evident.

Ronan picks up the bolt, his smile restored. "She will, once she experiences all of us."

It's not a bad plan. Satisfy the little human, pierce her, maybe even put a young in her womb by the week's end. By the time Zander makes his announcement, she'll be so thoroughly ours there can be no denying us our claim.

"It is too bad that the human males will not get to enjoy their own females." Ronan looks across the dome at a pair of humans laboring in the dry heat. They appear to be struggling.

I have personally never given them much thought. I shrug. "We need to concern ourselves with the survival of Zandia. Human DNA will live on here as well, so they may enjoy knowing that."

Ronan raises an eyebrow. "I hardly think it makes them rejoice."

I look again at the human men. They are much weaker than we are, unable to work as hard or as long, although they are certainly clever and have assisted well on the training pod.

"They will not be treated unfairly." To me, just allowing them to stay is a generous concession on Zander's part considering if the Ocretions ever find out we're harboring fugitives from one of their death pods, it could mean war. "And who knows. Perhaps they will find another species with which to mate, in the future." It's not my concern, in any case.

"Perhaps they will choose to relocate? Zander agreed to find them safe harbor on Jesel, where other human rebels are hiding out. That may be a place where they find mates some cycle in the future. Certainly, they will never get that here." Ronan begins to affix the bolt. "But enough of them. Let's take bets on how quickly we can get our female pregnant."

The thought of putting a young in that taut body of Riya's has me hard again. But taking on a mate will be more than sex. I'd better start researching how to manage a human female. Hasn't every Zandian who has one mentioned at some point how emotional they are? How they evoke long dormant emotions in our species? Already I see it in Tarren. She's under his skin.

Hell, she might already be under mine.

I'd better find out how to bond, discipline, and condition our female if we're going to make this bid for our future successful.

My cock surges against my uniform pants as I picture disciplining her. Stars knows I could find a million reasons to strip off her clothes, tie her up, and smack that gorgeous ass red. But will she like it? Rumor has it that they actually can get aroused by their discipline. Is it wrong that I hope Riya does?

But I'm getting way ahead of myself. The first task is to secure her as our mate.

R *iya*

Lily and I walk to the docked training pod after assisting in the new med dome, passing Zandian warriors and humans laboring all around the ruined capital. Some teams clean up rubble, while others erect more of the domes. Already the city appears nearly inhabitable, which is stunning, considering we were in battle just a planet rotation before.

I try to pretend I'm not looking for my three warriors.

Lily glances over my shoulder and lifts her chin. "Over there."

"What?"

"Your suitors—admirers. Whatever."

I can't stop myself from following her gaze and... damn. My breath catches. There they are. All three have removed their tunics, working bare chested, every row of hard muscle clearly defined under peachy-purple skin.

She bumps my shoulder and smiles. "It looked like they were giving you the hard sell in there earlier."

My face grows warm. "Hard sell. Yeah. You could say that. They just want a female for King Zander's rehabilitation project."

"Well, yes. But I would say they want *you,* in particular, to be their female."

I make a non-committal sound.

"So?"

"So what?"

"What do you think of them?" Lily prods.

My throat quivers. "Um... I'm not sure."

"They're cousins, I think. Rok says they're some of the best warriors Master Seke has trained. They're good-looking, don't you think?"

"I'm not interested," I lie. I refuse to look in their direction again, but my cheeks warm at my body's response to being cornered by them. Or—stars—the feel of Tarren's large hand on my ass. The way I ground my female parts shamelessly over his big thigh the previous planet rotation.

"I know you think they're handsome," Lily challenges me. "It's okay to look. You're in the pilot's seat, as far as I can tell."

We've walked past the place where the males are working, and it takes all my concentration not to slow my steps or turn back. "Oh really? How do you figure?"

"There aren't any available Zandian females. You're one of what? Maybe twenty-five females on the planet and they've determined we're compatible with their species. You're in high demand."

"Right, and they're in charge. Humans don't make demands in this galaxy or any other. Or have you forgotten?"

Lily shrugs. "I'm saying I think you have options. If you don't like those three, just show a little interest to another warrior and they'll be fighting over you."

"But either way, the story ends with me becoming a Zandian breeder. Getting claimed by not one, but multiple warriors for the purpose of continuing their species. Right?"

Lily puts a hand on my arm. "Zandians are honorable beings. They may be dominant and high-handed, but they're reasonable. This generation has been without females for years now and they're not used to humans. But believe me when I say that once the adjustment period is over, we're *very compatible*."

"And what if I don't want to mate at all? With any of them?"

Lily nibbles her lip, regret swimming in her green eyes. "I don't know. Humans aren't slaves here, but we are their guests. I think it will be *fall in line or leave*."

That's what I was afraid of.

Considering I was sentenced to death by my former slave masters and the barcode on the back of my neck would give that information to any being in the galaxy who scanned me, leaving isn't an option. Even if it was, I'd rather die now than go back to the agrifarm with the brutal slave masters. Which means spreading my legs for not one, but three huge horned aliens.

And I'd better hope to Mother Earth it takes them a long time to figure out there won't be any Zandian babies coming out of this womb.

Because I don't know what they'll do to me then.

R onan

"I'm first in the washtube," I holler the moment we finish our work, sprinting for the palatial pod.

"Ass," Jax mutters. I hear his feet pounding behind me, but I have the advantage of a head start. Besides, I'm definitely the fastest.

I make it to our shared chamber and bolt straight for the washtube, not stopping to take off my clothes until I'm standing in the middle of it and the door is closing.

I laugh as Jax pulls off a boot and hurls it at the closed door.

I made it into a game, but my sense of urgency is real. We have to get cleaned up and find our female.

I saw all the *vecking* gazes on Riya when she and Lily walked by and I wanted to beat each and every warrior to a pulp for even thinking about taking our female.

You might say I have a competitive streak. Good thing my cousins share it. I heard Tarren growling beside me and Jax wore that cool, calculating look that means trouble for anyone who gets in our way.

The way I see it, we need to get Riya in our hoverdisk—sleeping quarters—whatever by the end of this planet rotation.

The trouble is, the dark-haired beauty with a knockout body has guarded eyes. She's been damaged by males, so I'm sure as *veck* not going to force myself on her. I know Tarren and Jax wouldn't either. Tarren sounded like he wanted to find and rip the heads off whichever beings forced themselves on her.

But there isn't time to tread lightly, either. Teams need to be formed before King Zander makes his announcement. And the three of us know exactly nothing about winning over a female.

The washtube empties and I skip the drying phase, hitting the button to open the doors. "Your turn, beautiful." I grin at Jax as he passes me to step in. "Be quick, we have a female to court."

"You don't even know what *court* means," Tarren grumbles from his hoverdisk where he's sat down to remove his boots.

"Neither do you." I pad past him and pull on a fresh uniform in the crisp white of Zandia.

"So what's your plan, Master Romance?"

"I say we go find Riya and offer her a tour of the palatial pod. She's never been in it, right? She's probably curious. It's far more luxurious than the training pod she's used to. Maybe she'd prefer to stay here."

Tarren snorts. "You think it's going to be that easy? She'll just come to our chamber and stay?"

I grin. "I figure you and Jax will fill in the gaps of my plan."

Jax also cuts his shower short and emerges from the washtube. Tarren takes his place.

"That sums up your strategy on most everything," Jax observes drily, clearly having heard the entire conversation.

I shrug. "Good thing we get to share this experience, then, right?"

Jax gets dressed in his uniform. I recognize the thoughtful creases of his face and keep my mouth shut so he can think. I truly am grateful we're in this together, because I doubt I'd tempt a female on my own. I'm not as big as Tarren or as smart as Jax. I'm the one who makes beings laugh. But the way I see it, with my two cousins, we offer the full package. And I'm grateful for the chance to share a female with them.

Tarren emerges from the washtube.

"It's about *vecking* time. Let's go find our female," I say.

Tarren stalks naked through the chamber and grabs his uniform. "We should leave her alone. We're coming on too strong."

Jax folds his arms over his chest but doesn't answer. Experience tells me he's weighing our options.

"*Veck* that," I say. "Some other warrior is probably trying to stick his tongue in her ear right now." I pick my words carefully, guessing at what will get my cousin moving quickly.

I guess correctly.

Tarren growls and yanks on his pants.

"Or is that what you want?"

"That's probably enough goading," Jax warns me.

The three of us are out the door before I can count to ten. Tarren leads the way, hands curled into fists at his sides. Jax and I stalk behind him, sharing glances every time Tarren nearly knocks some being over.

We pass Master Rok and his mate Lily on the way out of the palatial pod and the three of us skid to a stop. There's a moment of awkward bows and formal greeting before Lily jerks her thumb toward the training pod. "Riya is in her chamber."

Jax straightens. Tarren's nostrils flare.

"Where do we find it?"

"It's a prison cell she shares with several other humans. Number 11 or 12, if I remember right," Lily explains.

We all drop at the waist for another round of bows. "Thank you, Lily, esteemed mate of Master Rok," I murmur.

Lily pulls a dagger from her sword belt and points at each of us in turn. "You force that girl into anything she's not willing to do and I'll personally cut your balls off. Understand?"

Rok's lips twitch, but he does nothing to subdue his female.

A muscle in Tarren's jaw jumps and his fists tighten. "*No being* will be forcing Riya," he growls.

"Especially not us," I add.

Lily gives a crisp nod and stows her dagger back in its scabbard. "Then good luck to you."

Rok chuckles as he leads her away.

The three of us exchange a glance as we exit the palatial pod and hike across the rubble to the training pod.

Jax curses under his breath when we walk through the training pod. It was once an Ocretion death pod, sent out to exterminate all the beings on it, so it's designed like a prison. Even though the cells have been made more comfortable with mats and blankets, it's still a *vecking* hell-hole.

To make matters far, far worse, the pod is *packed* with males. As we walk down the row of cells, we pass cluster after cluster of males crowding around females. Deep voices boast and taunt.

Ugh. If this is my species' form of courting, I'm a little less proud to be a Zandian this planet rotation.

When we reach cell eleven, it's no different. Five males are crowded in the cell with Riya and three other human females. She's backed in a corner, and the guarded mask she wore earlier has been multiplied by one hundred.

Her eyes lift to meet Tarren's when he shoulders his way through, making room for Jax and I to follow him in. He holds out his hand. "Come."

I want to elbow him for saying it like an order rather

than a request, but our female doesn't hesitate. She wants to be rescued. She stretches out her hand to grasp Tarren's, picking her way through the bodies to get to us. The moment she's close enough, Tarren swings her up into his arms.

Surprise brightens her face, but she doesn't protest, doesn't look back at the scene we leave. When we get down the corridor, and away from the oppression of male hormones and aggressive posturing, she kicks her feet.

"I can walk, you know."

"You will *never* walk when I can carry you," Tarren growls. "Not when there are other males sniffing around you like beasts."

"And I suppose you think you three are different?" There's a dryness to her tone that's particular to humans. I haven't learned all the nuances of their communication yet, but I think it's called sarcasm.

"You left with us, didn't you?" Jax challenges.

Her long-lashed golden eyes slide left to take in Jax. She purses her lips, but they've started to curve up. "Lesser of two evils," she mutters. "Will you please put me down?" She starts to struggle against Tarren again when we leave the pod. "Where are we going?"

"How would you like a tour of the palatial pod?" I offer, trying to make it sound like a real treat. "Have you seen the Great Hall?"

She stops squirming, relaxing into Tarren's hold. "No."

"Would you like to? It's quite beautiful."

"Only if I get to walk."

Jax smiles at our small victory. Tarren stops and drops her to her feet without a word or smile, still in gruff protector mode. I shudder to think what would've happened if we'd found another male touching Riya when we arrived.

My cousin is not to be challenged when he's serious about a fight.

Jax claims one of her hands, and I sweep in to grab the other, figuring Tarren already had his turn carrying her.

Jax and I start a running commentary on the finer points of the palatial pod as we enter, explaining some of the history of our species' survival after we escaped the Finnian invasion of our planet.

She walks along beside us, but I don't think she's listening.

She looks... worried. Which makes me want to pull her into my arms and soothe away her fears.

Does she think we're trying to get her into our chamber so we can take our turns with her?

Veck, that exact scenario is probably on all of our minds. Which means I need to come up with another tactic. Fast.

R *iya*

I wish the warriors would give me my hands back. My palms are clammy from nerves and I hate knowing I couldn't run away if I tried.

Ronan seems to sense my discomfort, because he's running his mouth at warp speed as if to distract me.

The trouble is, it only makes me more nervous.

These guys aren't like the Ocretion slave masters, but I have no doubt about what they want. Could they force me? *Yes.* Will they?

I remember Tarren's anger when he realized I'd been forced in the past.

No. I'm safe enough.

Not from their charm.

But that's crazy. I'm not actually going to *fall* for these males. That would be even more disastrous than agreeing I'm their mate. Because I won't get to keep them. Not after they find out I'm barren.

I stop walking. We took a lift to the main level and they've shown me all through the beautiful, opulent palace. Now we're in an empty corridor of a lower level, where I suspect their chamber must be.

"Listen." I pull my hands of out of theirs and place them on my hips. "You think you want me for your mate?" I look up at their handsome faces—their square jaws, smooth, hairless peachy-purple skin. Hungry eyes.

Three pairs of horns lean in my direction. Three males nod.

I shake my head. "I'm not the being you want. I won't make a good mate."

"*Veck* that," Jax says immediately. "You're ours."

I take a step back and my ass hits the wall. The three of them advance on me. "Y-you don't even know me. You don't know anything about me." I hate how much higher my voice sounds.

"I know you." It's Tarren who speaks this time, even though he's usually the silent one. "I know you're brave and stubborn."

I'm stunned momentarily by this observation. They're the last words I expected from his mouth.

"I know you're sensitive, despite your tough act. You care deeply for the beings around you, regardless of their species. You risked your life to save others during the battle."

My breath stalls in my chest. Tarren's gaze locks on mine and he pins me with it, right to the wall. He takes a step closer.

"So did you." My voice is hoarse.

My whole life I've been a barcode. I had human friends, yes, but I've never been seen as anything but a commodity.

I thought that's how Tarren and his cousins saw me, too.

Tarren lowers his voice and dips his head, bringing his sensual lips toward me until they hover just a whisper from my temple. "I know you blush when you think about me claiming you."

My panties dampen, pussy clenching at his words—at the heat of his skin, so close to mine. "I know the way your ass fills my palms."

I bite my lips to keep in the gasp. My buttocks clench, as if to remind me of how it felt to have him cupping my cheeks.

"I know the scent of your arousal." His gaze trails down to my breasts, where my nipples protrude through the fabric of my tunic. "I smell it now."

I can't hold back the tiny whimper that escapes my lips. I squeeze my quaking thighs together to alleviate the throb of my clit.

Ronan drags the hem of my tunic up slowly, as if I won't notice. When I try to bat his hand away, he just grins. It's an impish smile, one that puts me at ease, despite the audacity of his movements. "I just *have* to see your panties." He winks. "Just a peek, Riya?"

My face heats. I try to push his hand back down, but I can't stop the laugh in my throat. Stars, I never thought in a million years I'd giggle with a male over baring me.

The other two also grin—tentative smiles, like they're not sure if it's safe to relax yet.

"Come on Riya," Jax joins in, turning the full force of his persuasive charm on me. "Make our planet rotation. Show us the panties."

I must flush a deeper red, because my face feels like it's on fire. In fact, I cover my own eyes with my hand and surrender to their perusal.

A large hand drapes over mine, blocking all the light out. "Let me do that." It's Tarren.

One of them whistles—Jax, I think.

"Female, if you had any idea how badly we want to rip that scrap of fabric off your body and worship between those legs, you'd be covering more than your eyes right now." Jax's voice sounds deeper.

I want to pull my tunic down, but Tarren holds my hand firmly over my eyes, and Ronan still has the other captive.

"Give me this one," Tarren says softly and Jax transfers my wrist to Tarren's keeping. He adds it to the pile covering my eyes. "Don't move, Riya," he murmurs near my ear. His voice is gravelly. "Ronan's going to take a closer look."

I jerk when heat suddenly engulfs my panty-clad pussy, like Ronan's mouthing it through the fabric. There's a nip of teeth and more moist heat.

I squirm, unsure whether I'm trying to get away or get more.

"Do you want him to make you feel good, Riya?" That's Jax's voice, I think.

My head bobs around, the movement neither a nod nor a shake.

One of them thrums my nipples through my tunic. They're stiffer than Zandian crystal. "She wants it."

"No," I whimper, but I widen my stance, rock my pelvis

to meet Ronan's mouth. He groans and pulls my panties to the side.

The first lick of his tongue has me crying out. "Oh *veck*," he groans when he pulls away. "She tastes like glory."

Jax smothers a laugh but I don't hear the friendly ribbing he gives his cousin because Ronan returns to using his tongue between my legs, tracing it around my inner lips, flicking it over my clit.

One of them—probably Jax, reaches around and palms my ass, kneading one cheek as Ronan treats me to more flicks and licks that have me alternately rising to my toes and grinding over his mouth.

My legs tremble, honey leaks from my pussy. I've pleasured myself before, and I've been taken forcefully, but nothing in my life has prepared me for these sensations, this exquisite torture.

"Don't let her come." That firm directive comes from Jax and I stiffen, my tumble into release slowed. "Not until she agrees she's ours."

Ronan removes his tongue. Only his warm breath touches my throbbing clit.

"Ronan," I whine.

The hand on my ass tightens, like a warning. I remember again Tarren's threat to spank me the previous planet rotation. Do these males truly treat their women that way? With physical discipline?

Sweet Mother Earth, the idea shouldn't excite me so much.

"Who do you belong to, lovely?" Jax's voice has the cool patience of a teacher imparting a lesson.

Some stubborn part of me wants to say, *no male.* But I fear it's not true. If I refuse these males, Zander might assign me to others. What's more, I've already given in. They know it. I know it. I wouldn't be standing in the corridor with my tunic around my waist if I hadn't already agreed.

And dammit, I want to know what it's like to orgasm with a male's mouth on me. I never knew such a thing was done.

I sag against Tarren's hands holding mine to my eyes. "You. I belong to you three. Tarren, Ronan, and Jax."

All three of them rumble at once. There are muttered curses and hands tightening.

Ronan falls on my pussy like it's the one thing keeping him alive at the same time Jax curses and says, "You make it good. Reward our little mate every way you know how." He's squeezing my ass in one hand and pushes the other up my tunic to cup my breasts.

Tarren pulls my hands away from my face and claims my mouth. The thread of his stitches tickles my face as his lips slant over mine, possessive and hot.

He swallows my scream when Ronan sucks the little bud of my clitoris into his mouth. "Make her come," Tarren growls. "Teach her what to expect from us."

The words make me dizzy. Does he mean I can expect orgasms? Pleasure? Or just that my body will be used at their discretion all planet rotation long?

I'm not sure I care which meaning it was because Ronan wedges a thick finger into my opening and strokes my inner wall at the same time he sucks my most sensitive place.

I scream, throwing one leg over his shoulder, pressing my dripping pussy to his mouth as he tongues me over and over again until I reach the brink.

"*Ronan Tarren Jax*," I babble, my mind lost as I catapult into spasms of pleasure unwinding.

I sag into a chest—Tarren's—and I'm held up by more than one pair of strong arms. Ronan eases his fingers out.

Tarren swings me up off my feet again, this time to straddle his hip, the way a mother carries a child. "Let's get her to our chamber," he says. "I want to know what glory tastes like, too."

T*arren*

I carry Riya to our chamber and set her on her feet. The wariness returns to her face and her breath is quick, but her nipples still steeple the front of her tunic. And the scent of her arousal still fills my nostrils, making it hard to concentrate.

"We should pierce her," Jax murmurs, producing the small bag of crystals we've worked our entire lives to accumulate. The Zandian mating ritual involves piercing the bride with Zandian crystal to mark her as yours.

I nod, grateful for Jax's better functioning brain. Jax fishes through the bag, producing some of the smaller gems and holding them to the light to examine.

"Ronan, go get the equipment and anything else we need for a human mate."

Ronan hesitates. "What if we're not allowed to mate her? Do you think we need to petition first?"

"*No*," both Jax and I snap at the same time. Ronan's concerns are legitimate. But we've already decided it's better to claim her before any plans are announced.

"Right," he mutters. "I'll figure it out."

Riya swallows and takes a step back. To my dismay, she's turning pale.

Jax reaches for her twisted fingers and takes them into

his hands. "Piercing won't hurt. We'll numb the areas first—you won't feel a thing."

Tension radiates from her shoulders and I have the sense she's about ready to bolt for the door. "Wh-where will you pierce me?"

I can't stop the slow smile from spreading across my face. "Anywhere we want to, Riya."

Jax shoots me a *you're not helping* glance. "Where would you like to wear our crystal?"

Her fingers tug on an earlobe.

"Certainly there," Jax says smoothly, advancing on her. He brings the back of his index finger to brush over one of her nipples through her tunic. "How about here?"

She swallows. "I-I don't know."

I'm no good at soothing with words, so I do what I know. I pick her up, sit on my hoverdisk and settle her on my lap. Her body goes rigid at first, but gradually relaxes, the fresh scent of her arousal making my eyes roll back in my head with desire.

My body's response to having her soft ass resting over my cock is immediate. Her exotic scent—earthy and sweet—fills my nostrils. My cock strains painfully against my pants and my fingers splay around one of her firm thighs, pulling her tighter.

"Riya." My voice comes out sounding even deeper than normal. "We know you were mistreated before... badly. But you can trust us. If Jax says something won't hurt, he means it. Zandians don't lie."

Except for that one *vecker* we once called a friend. But I'm not thinking about him now.

I can't stop myself from going after one of her breasts. I palm it, squeeze it. I lean forward and scrape my teeth over her nipple. "It will give us pride to see you wearing our crystals." I'm already imagining her naked, bejeweled by us. It's making me crazy. I drag my gaze up from her breast and catch her chin in my fingers. "Tell me what you're afraid of."

She shivers and touches her eye. "I want to trust you. It's just... my experience with males has been bad. Extremely bad. Not just the shock sticks, but the..." she touches her eye again. "I don't know if I can be what you want, when it comes to, this." Her muscles are tight again.

Jax moves closer and burrows his fingers in Riya's hair. "We will not harm you, little female. We want to bring you pleasure, Riya."

She lifts her gaze to Jax's face and rubs her lips together. It's the same look she gave me in the medbay during the battle. When I had my hand on her ass. Vulnerability. Desire. Fear.

Ronan returns with a box of items and a broad smile.

"Any trouble?" Jax asked.

He shrugs. "Doctor Daneth wants to give her a full examination and gene test prior to mating, but I told him we didn't give two stars about the results of the test, she's the one we want."

I scent something salty and catch Riya blinking back tears. Alarm rockets through me. Is she that terrified?

But Jax puts a finger under her chin. "You see, pretty girl? You're the one we want."

She draws in a shaky breath and nods, squaring her shoulders. "Let's do this, then."

I'm loathe to move her from my lap, so I tug on her tunic until I free it from underneath her ass. "Lift up your arms," I command, and she obeys. I gently take the fabric and tug it over her head.

Veck, she's perfection. Her breasts are small and taut, the ripe buds of her nipples a warm peach. I palm both of them, causing Jax to growl.

"We want to look, too.'

I squeeze and knead her breasts, pinching the nipples until they stiffen even more. "I'm just readying her for you," I say gruffly.

Jax arches a brow and Ronan rolls his eyes, but they don't argue. Ronan sprays the same analgesic spray Riya used on me in the medbay over both her nipples, then onto his fingers to rub on her ear lobes. "Where else?"

I circle the rim of her belly button. "Here."

Ronan crouches down and I nearly groan, remembering the sounds she made last time he was between her legs. He lifts a brow toward the apex of her thighs. "Do we want to pierce her there?"

My cock screams *yes*, but Riya's gone rigid again.

Jax shakes his head. I give a nod of agreement.

Ronan loads the gun with our crystal and a bit of platinum wire to pierce her. I cage her hands in her lap with one hand and wrap the other around her waist to keep her from squirming. Ronan steps forward, but when Riya flinches, he hesitates.

Jax snatches the gun from Ronan and makes quick work of her earlobes. "You see?" He strokes his thumb down her pretty cheek. "It's nothing. Are you hurt?"

She shakes her head.

"Good. Pinch them for me, Tarren." He indicates her breasts.

With vecking pleasure.

I pull her hands behind her head and trap them there with one hand, then grip her breast with the other, lifting the protruding nipple in Jax's direction. Again, he's quick and deft with his movements, piercing her with an admirable efficiency. I change hands to offer the other nipple up and it's done.

"Now for the navel." Jax squats at our feet and runs his finger around the rim. "Top or bottom?" He's asking Riya, but I growl, "bottom" before she can answer.

"Is that agreeable, beautiful?" He flashes her his most charming smile. I don't know how he always maintains his easy, confident manner.

She gives a wobbling nod.

I squeeze a small section of her flesh below the navel for Jax's gun. In just a breath, he's pierced her there, too.

"Anywhere else?" He includes all of us in the question. "Somewhere else on the face?"

Riya gives an emphatic shake of her head and Jax chuckles. "All right, sweet thing. That's enough, then. Good girl. Thank you for your surrender."

"Not sure I had a choice," she mumbles, and I bristle, thinking of all the times her choice has been taken away from her. It makes me sick to think she'd put us in the same category as those Ocretion *veckers*.

"By the stars, do you think we're monsters?" I snap. I don't mean to sound so harsh. Jax flashes me a warning look but I plow on, "Did you not agree that we're your mates?"

She flushes, and I scent fear on her.

I'm instantly sorry. I soften my tone. "We've just won back our home planet. We want to share the satisfaction of rebuilding and making a home with a female. With *you*," I amend. "We don't wish to terrorize you."

Thank the one true Zandian star for my cousins, who step in to soothe her. "We're going to help you get over your past." Ronan holds out a hand and she takes it, standing up from my lap.

"After you've known pleasure with us, you'll never be afraid of sex again," Jax promises.

She swallows. "All right." Her voice is small. I hate seeing her diminished. It makes me swear anew to find every last asshole who hurt her and tear them apart.

But it's a start. She's agreed to let us try to please her. We can't ask for more than that.

R *iya*

I stare into Ronan's eyes. His handsome features are drawn into a look of need that makes my breath catch. I've never seen a being look at me, *Riya*, with such blatant desire.

I put a hand to my mouth and step back, bumping into Jax's strong body. He winds his arms around me and leans down to whisper into my ear. "Riya, I promise you will not find it so unpleasant." His breath is hot and sends wild tingles down my neck and to the tips of my nipples. Without thinking, I push backwards, grinding into his hips, to feel his hard length. *Hard* is the operative word, for sure. Even clothed as he is, I can tell that he has a large member, and suddenly, Lily's whispers about how wonderful mating is? It starts to make sense, at least to my body.

What's even better? He said my *name*. He named me, making me a person, not a possession. None of the Ocretion guards—that thought is swept away as he puts his lips to my neck and presses down, sending stars into my eyes and down my pulse.

"Relax into me," he murmurs and cups my breasts. He gently thumbs the new nipple rings and I flinch, even though the area is numb. "If these start to hurt, you be sure to tell us, all right, beautiful? Ronan will spray them again and take away any pain."

I nod and let my eyes flicker shut and drop my head back onto his strong chest, savoring his scent. I've never been held by a male before, never cared for. It feels so good to be in his arms.

Tarren's voice breaks into my reverie. "Let us move to the hoverdisk." His gruff tone, instead of putting me on edge, makes me eager for more of his touch as well. He may be rougher, but Jax was right earlier when he said I trust Tarren. Maybe it's because I saw him risking his life for humans and Zandians alike during the battle. Maybe it's because that shared trauma bonded me to him. For whatever reason, I do trust him.

I open my eyes and find him staring at me, and then he smiles. It's a wicked, feral smile, and it makes the stitches on his wound contort, but I love it. His lopsided grin is so gorgeous that I can't resist, and I smile tentatively back and hold out my hand. I've never done this willingly with one male, let alone three, but it feels right. His grip is warm and firm, and I squeeze hard, then shift my touch, sliding my small fingers along his long, strong ones. It still amazes me how powerful his species is, how large.

One of them rearranged the hoverdisks so that the three separate hoverdisks are now joined, making one enormous surface. Jax settles onto the mattress, leaning his back against the fabric on the wall, and holds me backwards against his chest. I feel his arousal between his legs, pushing against my buttocks. I wait for the sick feeling to take hold, the one I have any time I think about the male organ, but it doesn't come. When Jax holds my hips and tugs me harder into his body, the pressure of his malehood against my ass only makes me push back, wanting more.

Tarren steps forward, eyes glittering. "*Veck*, you're beautiful," he growls. "Wrap your arms around Jax's neck and hold on."

I obey. The position lifts and separates my breasts. My nipples peak in the air, even though it's not cold. My breath rasps in and out in short gasps as I watch him approach.

He kneels on the soft mattress. "Don't let go," he orders, then he leans in and puts his mouth to my nipple.

I don't expect to feel anything, since they've numbed the surface, but the sensation is like nothing I've ever experienced. I still can feel the warmth of his tongue, and when he sucks my stiffened nipple in his mouth, a shot of pure desire hits me at the juncture of my thighs. I shift, grabbing Jax's hair, and tug hard as Tarren suckles me, first on one side, then the other. When he bites down, I yelp at the sudden pop of pain, and then moan as the next feeling comes: desire.

"I think she likes that," Jax chuckles, stroking my belly, just above the area where I'm on fire. I make some kind of noise and push up, but that makes my nipples even more accessible to Tarren, who growls and bites the other one. He runs his hands down my thighs, squeezing, touching in the same rhythm his tongue uses on my nipples. Coupled with the way Jax is stroking my belly, soft, tickling brushes, it's making me both sweaty and needy.

"Oh!" I want more than I'm getting, although the sensation is almost too much.

"I think she needs to be bare," comments Ronan, his voice low and gravelly.

Tarren sucks hard on my nipple, then pulls back, letting

go with a pop of suction that makes me whimper anew. "Agreed." He swings his legs to the side and stands up. He helps me kick off my boots. "Lift your hips." He tugs at my panties. I obey and when I'm naked, Ronan taps my elbows.

"Let go of Jax now," he says, "and give me your hands." He pulls me up to a sitting position, then says simply, "Stand up. Let us see you."

He assists me to my feet and points to a spot on the floor. "Stand there, Riya." All of his usual joking playfulness is gone, replaced with a gritty, feral determination.

I don't know if it's fear or just resistance. Maybe I can't stand the humiliation of being naked while they're clothed. I shake my head and fold my arms across my breasts. "No." It was one thing to lie back with my eyes shut and let them touch me. This seems too intense. I won't do it.

Jax chuckles softly as he crawls off the hoverdisk. "Then we'll help you, lovely." He grips my wrists and pulls them over my head. He's so tall he can hold them fully stretched. Tarren and Ronan both circle me, taking their fill of my naked form. I should be angry, but instead I'm turned on. Like in the corridor, when Tarren covered my eyes, it's actually easier for me when they take control. Which makes no sense considering my history.

Still, there's no denying the arousal dripping onto my inner thighs.

Tarren steps up behind me and wraps one arm around my waist, splaying his fingers over my belly.

The belly that won't be growing large with Zandian babies. But I can't think about that.

His palm glides lower, then lower still, but before it reaches the place I'm dying for him to touch, his other palm smacks down on my bare ass.

"Spread your legs," Tarren says.

I don't move.

Jax pushes his boot between my legs and kicks my feet apart. "A little more obedience, beautiful," he says, but there's laughter in his voice. "Or else Tarren will heat that adorable ass of yours."

All three males inhale deeply.

Oh sweet Mother Earth. They can smell my excitement. *Damn their sensitive Zandian noses.*

Jax chuckles darkly. "I think she wants that." He burrows his fingers into my hair again and tugs my head back. His grip is not hard, but possessive. "Should we turn your pretty ass pink?" The pleasure in his voice reverberates around the room.

"No." It's less a word than a gasp and I already know it's useless. The matter has been decided. By my body as much as their desire.

"I've been dying to spank this ass since I first threatened it and watched your pretty face blush." Tarren nips my neck, his lips soft, teeth hard, and the mix of pain and pleasure makes me moan and try to push my body closer to his. "Don't worry. The pain will be worth it. Because, *veck*, I promise we know how to make you cry with pleasure, little mate."

Jax and Tarren both walk me over to the hoverdisk. Ronan sits on one side, and Jax on the other. Tarren, in the middle, adjusts me so my hips are over his lap, and my body is stretched out over the other two. Jax takes my hands, and Ronan holds my calves. Although I am naked, lying face downward, I feel surprisingly... safe. Like they will take care of me. Which is a strange feeling, since I'm about to be spanked.

"Spread her thighs a little," Tarren orders.

Ronan slides my legs apart. "Wider, Riya." He taps my

inner thighs, then slides his fingers along my skin, up and down, when I obey. "More." He helps me shift. "Good. Just like that, as wide as you can. This will be the position we like when you are to be punished."

My pussy clenches even as my face burns. Thankfully they can't see it. Jax squeezes my hands. "A little punishment always sweetens the pleasure," he promises.

I'm not so sure I agree, but I also can't bring myself to protest. The flutters in my belly wing with desire and heat and anticipation.

Maybe there is a bit of fear, because I blurt, "I'll obey you!"

Jax chuckles. "Of course you will."

Tarren—at least I think it's Tarren—rubs his palm over my ass. "Our punishment is not something to fear." He strokes, and at the same time, Ronan runs his fingers up my inner thighs.

"I don't know," Ronan's fingers trail closer and closer to where I need them. "I rather hope she disobeys often."

I never imagined I'd find punishment sexy, but I'm tingly everywhere and wet between my legs. For the first time in my life, I desire something only a male can give me. Only what *these* males can give me.

Tarren's palm crashes down on my ass and I squeal in shock. Pain blooms, a slow spreading fire across the offended cheek.

"Start her out lightly," suggests Jax, "Let her get used to the burn before you increase the impact."

I'm grateful for Jax's practical advice. I definitely want it lighter.

"If she takes it obediently, she might not even need the strap," suggests Ronan.

I nearly jackknife off their laps, my back bowing as my

head surges up. "*Strap*?" I twist to look over my shoulder at him.

Ronan laughs and shrugs, a slightly guilty expression on his face. "It would be fun, don't you think?" His fingers drift nearly to the cleft between my legs and flutter there, teasing me, where I am already wet. He chuckles when I squirm. "Riya, you think you're afraid, but your body has another idea."

"*Veck*, you're so wet," growls Tarren. "It's time to start this." He raises his hand, I feel the air draft, and then he slaps my other cheek. The impact makes a loud sound, and I cry out even though it doesn't really hurt this time.

He spanks me again. I wiggle.

"I see my handprint on your skin." His voice is low. "I'm going to turn you pink with spank after spank, Riya, so they all blend together to make your bottom glow."

I moan, and it's not clear to me whether it's from worry or pleasure, because the tone of his voice, and the tingle on my skin makes me press my hips down into his lap. I feel his hard length beneath me.

"Stay still," he orders me, and Ronan shifts to hold my thighs open more easily. His hands are strong, and although his grasp is not painful, it immobilizes me.

Tarren slaps me again, and again. It stings more, and I whimper.

"Are you done?" I cry out.

Tarren chuckles. "No, Riya. We're just getting started."

At that, he begins to spank me faster, a few times on each cheek in a row, and soon I'm bucking my hips furiously, trying to move away from the punishing blows. But Ronan holds me in place, and when I try to reach back to cover my ass, Jax tsks at me and squeezes my hands. "No, Riya," he says. "You don't get to determine when the

45

spanking is done. Hold my hands for support and accept the punishment."

"Get her upper thighs," Ronan suggests. "They're far too pale. You need to make them pink like her ass."

Tarren must agree, because next I feel his strong hand slap at the base of my buttocks, and it hurts far more. Even as the pain stings, there is something more, a growing need between my legs, and I start to anticipate each blow with as much eagerness as trepidation.

I'm almost in a reverie, when an especially sharp spank distracts me. "Ow!" I try to twist away. But with three strong warriors holding me in place, I have no chance to get away until they have decided it's enough.

Being restrained only increases the wicked heat between my wet thighs, a heat that is already matching the burn on my ass, and I wiggle. "No..." I whisper, but I'm humping Tarren's lap.

Tarren's hand crashes down harder, matching the intensity of my need and I arch back to meet it.

Tarren gives a harsh curse and the spanking stops. I lie panting, feeling the heat from all three of their bodies, and exultation rolls through me at the way they are using my body in ways I never could have dreamed would be exciting.

Tarren strokes my ass now, soothing the wicked burn he put there, and as he does it, Jax massages my forearms, and Ronan starts playing his fingers up my inner thighs. I arch back, spreading my thighs wider, dying for him to finally touch me where it aches.

He finally does, brushing ever-so-lightly over my dewy petals.

I buck, trying to bring my hips closer to his fingers. I fight to get my hands back from Jax, but he only laughs and grips my hair, lifting my head for a kiss.

It's an awkward, misaligned, *hot* kiss. I whimper into his mouth at the same time Ronan finally gives me the full weight of his fingers. He strokes firmly along my weeping slit and groans.

"She's so wet and..." He drags his fingers to the side and nudges my thigh wider, pulling my buttcheek out of the way. "Feel this." His voice is laced with awe. "Feel how plump and ripe she got." He strokes again, and the coil of desire ratchets tighter.

I hear a growl and a second hand plunders between my legs. Must be Tarren. He groans. "I need to see it," he mutters, not stopping the long strokes. "I need to see it *now*."

It's Ronan who directs the group this time. "Lie her back again, as before, on Jax." He helps me off their laps and points to the hoverdisk, where Jax has already arranged himself against the headboard

I find myself once again nestled in Jax's arms, sitting between his thighs. My ass tingles with heat and residual sting but soon I forget about that as Tarren comes forward and spreads my legs, placing them on top of Jax's, so that I'm open wide, my sex on display. I don't resist for a second, because I'm dying for him—for them. In fact, I open my thighs as wide as I can in this position and moan as Jax reaches around my body and begins to tease my nipples with his fingers.

I'm not sure how Tarren is going to mount me, but my breath catches in my throat as he slides his body down the hoverdisk until his face is just above my hips. "Are you ready?" His voice is hoarse with need. It's then that I realize he plans to put his mouth onto me, as Ronan did in the corridor, and I want it so badly I could cry.

"I'm..." I say, and then all that comes out is a sort of whimper as his hot tongue touches my clit. The feeling is so good, just so incredible—never in my self-explorations have my own fingers drawn this kind of sensation from my body.

I close my eyes and push back into Jax's chest, trying to use him as leverage to push my hips up to Tarren's mouth. "Oh!" He flicks my clit with his tongue and the feeling floods me at once. "Tarren." I reach forward to tug at his horns. They harden and lengthen in my hands and Tarren lets out a roar.

Jax squeezes my nipples hard enough to make me squeak. "No," Jax tells me. "If you do that, Tarren's going to lose control and *veck* you until you scream, and Ronan and I still want to enjoy you."

As if to affirm Jax's words, Tarren licks and sucks me like his life depends on it, making me squeal and squirm.

"I'll hold her hands." Ronan comes to my side. "Riya, put your hands behind Jax's head again."

I do it, barely able to understand words at this point, because Tarren holds my thighs, one in each strong hand, and begins licking along my cleft, all the way from my buttocks to my clit, over and over. I try to wiggle—first it's too much, then I need more, but he holds me down, making me take every flick and swipe, exactly where he wants it.

Jax plays my nipples harder, rolling the new studs until it hurts, then touches them softly, grazing his nails over the tips until I writhe against him.

Ronan bends over, squeezing my hands, and bites my neck in a spot that drives me wild. And now, with the triple sensation, hands and mouths touching me, licking, flickering, I can't hold it back anymore, and the most phenomenal orgasm starts to build in my core.

"I'm going to..." I shudder.

"No." Tarren looks up at me, his eyes flashing, his lips slick with my juices. "Not until you receive permission."

Confusion clouds my brain. Didn't they promise me pleasure? Why would they hold it back? "But please!" My whole body is keening for release.

"Just a little longer. Show us how you want to please your mates." Ronan reaches between my legs with one finger, swirling it around in my moisture as Tarren continues to lick.

Surprisingly, I *do* want to please them. "Yes, please," I beg.

Ronan chuckles. "Tarren, she's not going to last much longer no matter how hard she tries."

I can't hold it back any longer, and Tarren must realize it. "Riya, you may come." I do. With a strangled cry, I allow the pleasure to burst over me like a thousand bolts of lightning, seeing only white flashes behind my eyelids. I contort and moan and come, gloriously, into his lips. It seems to last forever, and finally, once the peak is over, I flop back into Jax's arms, trembling with the aftershocks, unable to move.

Tarren growls and pulls himself up to lie beside me, still in Jax's arms. He splays his hand protectively over my belly, rubbing my mound softly as I come back to myself.

Jax's hands have stilled on my breasts, and now he strokes me gently, on my arms and chest. Tarren's mouth is gentle on my neck, and I sigh in utter pleasure, totally comfortable, feeling safe and protected—and sated—in a way I've never experienced in my entire life.

If this is what it means to be mated to three Zandians? I don't mind it. I might even love it. I shift, feeling the slight tingle in my ass from the punishment, and instead of distress, the only urge I feel is one of arousal.

After a few minutes, Jax nips my neck. "Enough rest. Your mates won't last much longer looking at that beautiful body without claiming you. And believe me, you want us controlled when we take you for the first time."

I suck in a breath. Are they all going to take me *at once*?

Jax chuckles, possibly reading the alarm on my face. "Would you like to give Ronan or Tarren pleasure the way they gave it to you?"

"Ronan." Tarren orders and gives his cock a rough squeeze over his pants. "He can have her mouth. I need all of that sweet, wet pussy."

Said anatomy contracts at Tarren's possessive growl. I sit up, but I have to admit I'm daunted. I don't really know what I'm doing. I've never been with a male willingly before. Never wanted to give pleasure until now. "I..."

As if Jax guesses at the cause of my reluctance, he says, "We'll help you, Riya. All you have to do is obey." He lifts me easily from the hoverdisk.

R *onan*

I don't know how I got so damn lucky to be the first one to taste her and now the first one to spend, but I'm not going to argue. Tarren wants her pussy. I think her mouth is *vecking* perfection.

I strip quickly out of my uniform.

"On your knees." Jax guides her gently down. I'm thankful for the rug on the floor which is soft and plush, with enough cushioning to make kneeling comfortable for her. "Put your hands behind your back until you're told otherwise."

All three of us make a sound of approval when she assumes the position. Putting her hands behind her back lifts and spreads her breasts. Her pierced nipples stand out in stiff points and they're even more beautiful with the precious gems that now adorn them. *Our* crystals. Forever marking her as ours.

"Spread those knees a little, let us see that pink center that's driving us all wild," Jax tells her.

She obeys. Her eyes are glassy with desire, lips swollen from our kisses. I was going to tell Jax to shut his *vecking* mouth, but she seems relieved to have the instruction. I suppose even a tough little female like her might be nervous when she doesn't know what to do. No chance of doing something wrong or failing. But she still seems nervous, and I'm gutted when she darts a look of supplication at Jax.

He offers an encouraging smile. "Ronan will direct you if he wants. But except for using your teeth, you can't do it wrong."

My heart pounds against my chest at the realization that she's nervous about *pleasing* me. The scent of her natural lubrication grows stronger, and she even makes a little noise of desire. I settle in front of her, thighs spread, my cock harder than a *vecking* stone. She stares at the tip where a drop of pre-cum beads it.

Her eyes widen. "It's rainbow colored."

I grin. "What color did you think it would be? Purple, like our blood?"

She flushes. "I just didn't know."

She appears fascinated. "May I..." she reaches out a hand, then hesitates, probably remembering Jax's order.

"*Veck*, yes. Touch me, Riya," I growl. My body is tight with need, my muscles clenched and my member hard and throbbing.

She wraps her small hand around my cock. Her fingers don't even come close to closing around my width.

I can see she looks daunted, so I take my cue from Jax and give her instructions. "Grip tightly," I order, shuddering when she does. "Rub up and down while gripping, from the head to the base. Like that. *Yes.*" I'm quickly going to lose the ability to speak at all because I've never been so turned on in my life. I groan, and my eyes flicker shut.

I fight to catch my breath. "Now lean forward and put your mouth onto the tip, Riya. Lick with your tongue over the top and sides while you keep rubbing up and down." I'm telling her the way I've imagined it my whole life, which doesn't mean I've ever had it this good.

We've paid for females in intergalactic brothels before, but this is totally different. She's our *mate*. I'm training her to serve me. I'm going to learn what makes her scream.

When she touches the tip of her tongue to my cock, I groan again, louder than before. She doesn't seem to mind my taste, because she licks again and again over the tip, encouraging my body to leak more fluid. I'm surprised with how quickly she gets comfortable, lifting her beautiful golden gaze to my face to watch for my reaction as her clever tongue makes my balls draw up tight, and my cock strain for release.

She starts twisting a little when she squeezes and allows saliva to coat her fingers to make her palm slick, and I nearly combust. Within moments, I'm ready to come, my thighs tight and shaking and my breathing fast.

"Oh stars, take me deep," I beg, my voice taut. "All the way into your throat."

I press my throbbing member to the back of her throat. At first, she gags a little and has to pull back, but I stroke her hair, encouraging.

Then I can't stand it anymore. I grip the back of her head and urge her over my cock. I set a rhythm, pushing her down, allowing her up. Her eyes tear up when I hit the back of her throat, and I curse but still I can't stop. Instead I stroke my thumb over her cheek to thank her, to soothe her, even while I still control the movement of her head, faster and farther. "*Veck*, Riya, I'm going to come in your mouth." My voice is ragged. "Can you swallow it, sweet girl?"

She murmurs in agreement before I push into her throat roughly, and my cock swells even more.

"Riya," I shout as I come.

She swallows, again and again, eyes wide with alarm. I finally get command of myself and pull back to let her suck in air.

"Stars, yes," I roar, as I finish coming.

She drags her hot little tongue up the length of me and pops off, a smug smile in place. I *vecking love* seeing her pleased with herself.

I moan and lie back onto the hoverdisk, panting, my whole body going limp with the release. "*Vecking stars,*" I exclaim. "I never knew it could be so good."

R *iya*

Satisfaction soars through me, and a tenderness I never expected. Damn. I need to keep my emotions out of this. I can't fall in love with these males because some planet rotation soon I may have to leave this—them.

But there's no time for those thoughts, because Tarren

lifts me to my feet. "My turn," he growls, backing up and sitting on the edge of the hoverdisk.

Jax doesn't protest, he only looks amused, which is a relief. I'm not sure what I would do if the males started fighting over me.

Somehow Tarren's removed his clothing while I was sucking Ronan off and *holy Earth*. He's a giant, ripped with muscles so defined I could use them as handholds to climb.

"I want you straddling my lap," he growls. "Like the previous planet rotation in the medbay."

Thrills of excitement wing through me. He's remembered the scene with as much desire as I have. But when he grips the base of his shaft, I freeze just before I swing my leg over his rock-hard thighs.

Damn.

If I thought Ronan was big, Tarren is a beast. How am I ever going to fit him in?

"I brought lubricant," Ronan offers, still sprawled on his back on the hoverdisk watching. He points to the box he came in with.

Jax gets up and rummages through it, holding up items that should give me worry. A leather paddle. A strap. A cane. Some huge phalluses. A bottle of lubricant with a pump. He tosses it to Tarren, who wastes no time in dispensing it and swathing it over his huge member.

My chest gets tight. Memories of being forced flash through my head.

Jax comes up to stand behind me, hands on my shoulders. "Easy, Riya. There's nothing to be afraid of. He's putting you on top. You know what that means, don't you?"

I bite my lip trying to stuff down the irrational terror that has me shaking. I try to focus on Jax's words, because I know they make sense. I nod. Tarren's giving me the control. I'll be on top.

Tarren opens his large arms and I stumble forward, falling into him. In a moment, I'm straddling his lap, just as he asked, but it feels more like an embrace. My face is tucked into his neck and I'm breathing in his scent.

His cock twitches and I realize I'm right up on him, my clit pressing down on the base of his impressive length, which juts up between us. "This is how badly I wanted you the previous planet rotation," he says when he catches me looking between our bodies." He palms my ass and pulls me tighter, which has the effect of dragging my clit over his hard flesh.

I gasp.

"Go ahead, little girl. Rub that juicy pussy all over my malehood. This is what you wanted to be doing back in that medbay, wasn't it?"

I flush, but I know he's right. My body exalts in the pleasure of grinding down, satisfying the growing need between my legs.

He kneads and squeezes my ass, helping me rock over him. "I couldn't keep my hands off you, could I?"

I close my eyes and lose myself to the sensation, the pleasure blooming hotter and hotter in my core.

"You were so *vecking* magnificent out on that battlefield, trying to drag the bodies in all by yourself."

I open my eyes and look at him. It's the second time he's talked about me. Really about *me*. He sees beyond the choosing of a breeder for Zandian babies.

Needing to give him something back—or maybe just to satisfy my own needs, I don't know anymore—I reach down between us and tuck the head of his enormous cock into my entrance.

He's big, but it feels so right. Like perfection. My natural lubricant mixes with the one he applied, and he slides in a little more when I rock forward.

We both groan.

Jax reaches around and palms my breasts, and I buck, taking another few inches. "Show us how you wanted to please yourself with Tarren last planet rotation," he murmurs in my ear.

It's all the encouragement I need. As three pairs of eyes, all burning with lust and appreciation watch me, I impale myself on Tarren's cock, taking him as deep as I can.

His fingers tighten on my ass with a bruising force, but I love it—I love every moment of seeing these males come undone because of what I do to them. What we're doing is so different from my past that I stop drawing comparisons. This is passion. It's communion. It's an exchange between willing players.

I drop my head back and moan, letting Tarren move my hips. He goes slowly at first, like I'm made of glass and might break, but each time he pulls me over his cock, it gets easier to take him. I stretch and let him fill me. He can't get his full length in, but he doesn't seem to mind. His lips draw back to bare his clenched teeth and his arms shake with the effort of holding back.

"*Veck*, Riya. *Veck, veck*," he growls. "I'm not going to last more than a minute in your perfect little pussy."

That does it for me. My pussy clenches and I catapult over the edge into a release even more satisfying than the last two. My internal walls squeeze and spasm around Tarren's hard length and he roars, yanking me over his cock, ramming so deep it hurts. His hot essence fills me as I fall against his chest, panting for breath, digging my fingernails into his shoulders.

The rest is a blur. Tarren's holding me tight. I'm lifted and rearranged horizontally, my body snuggled up against his. Another body tucks in behind me. I'm drifting on bliss, comfortable and safe between my warriors.

Just before I fall asleep, it occurs to me that Jax hasn't had his turn. "Jax?" I murmur, opening my heavy lids.

"I'm here, lovely."

Jax is the one I most have to watch out for. The one who reads me so well. He's not either of the males I'm sandwiched between, which worries me. I attempt to sit up.

"Is it your turn?" I mumble sleepily.

He chuckles and leans over me, kissing my temple. "Later, sweet girl. Rest up for me."

My eyelids flutter, but I can't keep them open. I slide into the most blissful sleep of my life.

3

Jax

I bring food to our chamber for Riya when she wakes, but our sweet female has hardly moved since the planet rotation before. She's tucked up against Tarren's chest, Ronan spooning her from behind. My cousins are awake but seem loathe to move from the hoverdisk—or hoverdisks, plural, since we shoved the three beds together to make one large pallet.

Riya is *vecking* beautiful in sleep, her cheeks flushed, full lips soft. There's a line between her brows that even slumber hasn't erased, though, and it makes me even more determined to learn her fears and erase them one by one.

"Prince Zander—I mean, King Zander, has called another gathering this afternoon," I tell my cousins.

Tarren scowls at me because my voice makes Riya stir.

Ronan catches the tension in my voice, though, and sits up. "What about?"

"About the rehabilitation plan. And repopulation. About

Zandian brides." Was it only the planet rotation before when he'd announced they were working on something? Somehow, I thought things would move more slowly. Teams are still out sweeping the planet for any remaining Finn.

But, of course, there's no time to waste. He wants us out there rebuilding for precisely that reason—to occupy the entirety of the planet and ensure the domination of our species, meager in numbers though we are.

"Why are you worried?" Riya asks.

She sits up and both Tarren and Ronan pull her back down, stroking her skin, soothing her. But her eyes are trained on me.

I shrug. "There's some talk about gene tests to determine partnerships. Dr. Daneth has some gene matching program. But we're all right, because we're already mated." I say it, but until Zander approves our match and gives us a homestead, I'm going to stay alert.

My cousins seem to understand my subtext, which is unfortunate, because the crease between Riya's brows gets deeper. She tries to sit up again and this time my cousins let her.

"I brought you some food, lovely. Humans must eat several times a planet rotation, isn't that right?"

Her shy smile cracks my chest open wide. "Yes."

I bring the tray of food over, but she's already climbing over Tarren, who flashes me a pained look when she brushes his rapidly growing erection.

"I'm just going to run to the washroom," she says.

We all watch the motion of her bare ass as she walks, and Ronan grabs his cock and groans.

As soon as the door slides shut, Tarren asks, "They wouldn't take her from us, would they?"

I rub my jaw. "I don't think so. We claimed her. She's wearing our crystals. That's as good as Zandian law."

"King Zander writes Zandian law," Tarren says drily. "He could change it to fit his repopulation plan."

I shake my head. I haven't even physically claimed her yet, but there's no changing my mind. "She's ours. We'll have to make him see that. He's a reasonable ruler."

My cousins nod in agreement.

I hear the sound of the washtube starting in the washroom and the thought of Riya's naked body under the spray has me moving before I even know my own intent.

My turn.

Veck yes. It's my *vecking* turn. I've been more than patient to claim my female. I hit the button on the washtube to stop it, grinning when the door slides open revealing a dripping and surprised Riya. I strip quickly and crowd her back into the tube, then restart the water fill.

"Did you think you'd clean off my cousins' cum before I've had a chance to spill in you?

"I was cleaning for you." Her voice is husky even though her eyes are wide with shock, probably based on the force with which I've captured her against the washtube wall.

My raging hard-on throbs at her words. I knock her legs open with my knee, let her feel the state of my agony press up against her most sensitive parts. "Well, I can't *vecking* wait, lovely. I've waited too long already and now you're the being who will pay."

Her breath sucks in, eyes dart in micro movements to focus on my face, which is looming over hers.

"You think I can *vecking* be gentle with you now, sweet Riya?"

I know I'm being an ass, but I can't stop myself. I'm too far gone with lust, with need. If I don't *veck* this female soon

I will explode. I collect her wrists and pin them above her head, swallowing her gasp with my mouth. I kiss her like I want to devour her, lips, tongue, teeth all claiming and abusing her mouth.

Some rational part of me fights to the surface. Riya's been abused too many times. I break the kiss, backing up to check on my little human. Her eyes are glazed with lust, lips swollen. She pants, staring at me dazedly.

I shove my hips up against hers, my cock blindly seeking her entrance. "You're not afraid of me, are you, little female?"

She hesitates, but then shakes her head.

I have to go further. To really be sure. "You want this?"

This time, there's no hesitation before she nods.

Thank *veck*.

I groan and fist my cock, rubbing the head over her juicy slit. Her flesh plumps, guiding me—no, practically *sucking* me in.

It's been ages since I've had a female, and it's not like we've had any experience beyond the rare intergalactic prostitute. I groan at the utter ecstasy of being inside her. I don't know how my cousins stood it without pounding her to bits.

"Riya," I rasp, my lips against hers, my torso smashing her against the washtube wall. Water fills up all around us, about to engulf our heads, and I don't care, all I know is Riya. Sweet Riya. I cover her mouth with mine and thrust, lifting her off her feet with the force. Her legs come up to wrap around my waist and I palm her ass to drill into her. I hardly notice the water drain, the light spray of aromatic oil that coats our bodies. It makes her all the more slippery.

"I won't last long. I need you"—I slam in deep and hard, sliding her up the shower wall—"too"—another brutal thrust—"much." My voice doesn't even sound like mine—it's deep and raspy.

I lose my mind completely. I meant to care for her needs, to make sure she received pleasure, but I'm too far gone. I jackhammer into her like my life depends on it. My hands slip on her ass and one of my fingers slides in her crack.

Her muscles tighten, and I shout.

I'm coming like a battleship in warp speed, but our beautiful human is, too. I press on the little ring of her anus since that seemed to be what set her off and she squeezes even tighter, milking every last drop of cum from my cock.

"Beautiful girl," I murmur against her neck when I'm able to breathe again. I tap her anus again and her muscles tighten again. "I'm glad you like my finger there, because that's where I'm going to take you next time." I prop my knee up to hold her pinned to the wall and stroke both cheeks of her ass. "Thinking about *vecking* this tight little ass of yours has been driving me wild."

Her muscles squeeze again, even though her whimper sounds a touch afraid.

"Don't worry, sweet human. You can trust us to make it good for you. We love to hear your moans of pleasure. See your face when you crest the peak."

She ducks her face and hides it against my shoulder and I chuckle, reluctantly lowering her feet to the shower stall and slipping out of her.

Her arms drape around my neck and she doesn't drop them, which rearranges my heart in my chest. "You will get to keep me, right?"

Damn. She overheard our conversation. "Yes," I say firmly.

"Even if—"

When she stops, I disentangle her arms so I can look at

her face. Something's bothering her and I need to know what it is so I can fix it. "What?"

"What if I'm not the best breeder for you? Not the right gene match? What if I don't get pregnant at all?"

I want to follow up with more questions—figure out what has her worried, but her beautiful golden eyes fill with tears, and my priority becomes comforting.

I pull her against my chest and burrow my fingers in her wet hair, massaging her scalp. "We don't care if you're the best gene match, Riya. We've already chosen you. And you've accepted us. You're wearing our crystals, lovely. The king won't deny our claim on you. There's nothing to worry about."

Her body shudders as she drags in a breath, but when she pulls away her eyes are dry. She gives a brave nod and steps out of the washtube, which has been standing open.

I give her ass a slap, just because it's irresistible. "Go eat the food I brought you and report for duty. We'll see you this afternoon in the plaza for King Zander's announcement."

"Yes Master," she murmurs. It's an automatic reply, one conditioned into her by a lifetime of slavery, but it goes right to my dick. I know it's wrong—I should tell her I'm not her master, we're her mates, but I love the submissive reply too much.

I watch her naked form sashay into our chamber and have to bite my knuckle. My cock's standing erect again already.

I'm never going to get enough of our little mate.

R *iya*

I can't find my mates in the crowd—there are too many beings thronged in the plaza and I arrived late, because one of the humans was in critical condition and required a surgery. Dr. Daneth is unaccustomed to performing surgeries—apparently Zandians don't require much medical care—so it was a stressful shift with all of us standing at the ready to assist him.

King Zander turns to his gathered subjects and raises his hands, and every being falls silent in respect for their leader.

After sharing a special smile and nod with his mate Lamira, who holds his infant son, Zander clears his throat and activates a voice amplifier. It carries the sound all the way across the broken plaza. "My loyal subjects and honored guests." He makes eye contact with each Zandian and human in turn. "I am proud to stand before you this planet rotation to announce we are ready to engage in the next phase of Zandian rehabilitation, repopulation, and renewal."

Cheers break out, and Zander holds up a hand for silence. "In order to protect our planet from a new invasion and be sure we have rooted out all infestation of the Finn, we must settle the entire planet. It is a daunting task considering our current numbers, which is why we are implementing a homesteading plan. Our engineers have tested and are satisfied with the DomePod systems, which will allow us to quickly and easily create homesteads. Teams will be assigned an area of land in which to erect a dome.

Each dome will be comfortable, with all the luxuries

you deserve. Some of the lands of Zandia were untouched by the Finn and remain pristine. Unfortunately, these are not the areas we are concerned with. Where we need help most is in the over-mined areas. You will be responsible for replanting native plants as well as food crops from Earth to sustain our human population."

Again, the king sends a special look to his bride, and my heart constricts. Perhaps the Zandians truly are willing to partner with humans rather than rule us.

"Each team will manage crops and make the land fertile. They will also leave their homestead to help create roads, and other infrastructure for our soon to be growing population."

The area buzzes with low chatter and questions.

How will you pick the teams? Can we choose the location of our dome? Will we get mates? Will we find more Zandians for our planet?

Zander holds up a hand and the crowd instantly falls silent. "You have many valid questions. We believe there are pockets of Zandians around the galaxy who are either trapped, enslaved, or unable to reach us. We will continue to search for them. However, on our planet, repopulation is critical to our survival. As you can see," he gestured around the room, "Of our unmated females, we have no Zandians, and few human females, compared to many Zandian males. This is not ideal for growing our population."

Even though I know this is coming, my stomach tightens.

"And therefore," the king continues, "I have worked with my advisors to develop a new plan. Zandian males who are interested may volunteer for the homestead project. Groups of two to five Zandian males and at least one female mate will be teamed up and each will be assigned their own dome to manage, protect, and enhance the area. Those who stay for a minimum of five solars will then own the land on which they settled."

He pauses for emphasis. "We will use a new DNA matching program to select the best possible genetic matches for healthy offspring. The female will mate with all of her males, and, star willing, bear many healthy young over the years."

The chatter grows louder, every being looking around, exclaiming in surprise, and, like the previous gathering, eyeing all of the unattached females with great interest. Even though I've been claimed, I cross my arms over my chest and begin to breathe rapidly.

Zander stands taller, and there is silence. "I will say this, to both Zandians and humans. In an ideal society, you would get to choose your mate, or mates, yourself, and at some point in the future, I am confident that we will achieve that again on Zandia. At the moment, you are our valued pioneers, our soldiers, our explorers. You are the ones whose hard work and sacrifice will be listed in the history holos that generations of Zandian children will view hundreds of years from now. You are our heroes. And the hero's path is not always easy. Know that I, and the future of this planet, honor your sacrifice."

He bows his head to the crowd, like this is a sacred and meaningful moment, and I see more than one being bow their head back in reply. I guess it would be wrong for me to snort or roll my eyes.

"I thank each of you, Zandians and humans, for entering into this agreement with me and with our future to keep Zandia alive."

The Zandians lift their fists in the air, elbows bent at ninety-degrees in their traditional salute.

But nerves tighten in my belly. If King Zander insists on gene matching, he'll discover I'm barren. The Zandians may then have no use for me.

And even if they did have some other use, I can't deny the stab of pain that thought produces. I don't want to leave my mates. I'm not ready to give up the pleasure and attention they've already brought me.

"If a human female does not approve of her mates, she may petition for a change. Zandians, as well, can apply for a change if their human is not compatible. However, there is little room for choice at this point in our rehabitation. Humans must be sponsored by Zandians to ensure our culture and rules continue as the dominant one on our planet. Because I have no doubt more and more humans will find their way here as refugees or through our purchase for breeding."

Again, he darts a glance at his bride. It's commonly known he bought Lamira for breeding based on the gene matching test he wants to do on all of us now.

"And we will only continue to provide humans with a secure place in the galaxy if they agree to integrate to our society. Follow our rules." His voice sounds compassionate but firm. "Humans, you have earned your freedom with your assistance during the war, but freedom here comes with obligations and expectations to help rebuild our planet. By accepting this role, you are helping save our race, and yours, from extinction, and I am honored to have you participate. If you do not choose to join us in this endeavor, we will find you the best possible position on another planet."

Now I almost do snort. Every being in the crowd knows what that means—either going back to a factory or an agri-farm as a slave, working as a sex slave, or being a personal pet—all of which are fraught with more danger and horrors than anyone is willing to risk. And considering almost all the non-Zandians had been sentenced to death and were rescued from the Ocretion death pod, leaving would mean certain death.

"Human females—you will accept your mates, and work with them to make your dome a successful, thriving part of Zandia. Zandians—treat your female with the utmost respect and honor. She will provide us with the ultimate reward—our future. You may see Dr. Daneth for training on best practices for breeding and discipline. Above all, you will keep her safe."

My belly flutters at the word *discipline*. I experienced a little of their form of discipline the past planet rotation, but I'm sure my mates could be far more... *impactful* if they'd wanted to be. I imagine that's why Ronan returned from the doctor's lab with the box of sexual devices and implements of torture. My sight goes dizzy for a moment before I take a deep breath.

Lily appears beside me and leans in. "Are you all right?" she whispers.

"I'm fine." *As long as they don't gene test me.* I can't get sent away; I will need to make this work.

"Are you worried about the discipline? It isn't the shock-sticks of the agrifarm. It's—" she flushes, lowering her voice to a near whisper, "intimate and sexual."

Oh, I know all about it. My belly flutters again, a wetness growing between my legs. My face grows warm. I shake my head.

Lily still thinks I'm worried about discipline. She tilts her head. "Oh they're dominant—you'll have to follow their rules or suffer the consequences, but sometimes the consequences are worth it." She grins.

"Well you just have one dominant warrior giving your orders. I'll have three."

Her smile stretches wider. "Three warriors to pleasure you at the same time."

I can't help but grin at her waggled eyebrows. "It's like you're the one who wants three mates. What if I told Rok?"

"Oh, Mother Earth, he'd tie me to the hoverdisk and take his sword belt to my ass if I told him I wanted more mates!" She rolls her eyes at my shocked giggle. "That's the part of this rehabilitation plan that I fear will fail. Zandian warriors are possessive. It's hard to imagine how they'll learn to share one female. But I suppose if Zander orders it, they'll follow. They are nothing if not loyal subjects."

I think about my three mates. They hadn't appeared to be competing with each other. But they're cousins. Maybe they're used to sharing. It's another point in their favor, not that I'm tallying.

"Just think, you'll have three warriors utterly devoted to you. Three to take care of you."

Before now, I've never had even one being take care of me. But she's right. The males did take care of me, even though I had little say in how things went. Just for argument's sake, I play devil's advocate. "Three warriors as my slave masters."

"You're not a slave anymore," Lily urges. "I mean, not *really*. It's different—you'll have some choice. You heard what the king said. If they can't make it work, you can petition for new mates. You'll see." Her eyes, when they meet mine, dance with empathy and something else—a confidence.

If she only knew I share her confidence about my mates. It's whether I'll be able to *keep* them as my mates that scares the crap out of me.

I search the crowd for them. I've been looking since I arrived, and now I see them, elbowing their way to the front. Ronan looks right at me and gives me the most dazzling smile. Relaxation washes over me, like everything is going to be fine. As his smile turns wicked, the relaxation morphs into arousal.

How can it be these males already trained my body to respond at the sight of them? This morning in the wash-tube, I thought I should be afraid of Jax, the way he came at me with so much aggression. But instead his passion made me feel powerful. To know that he couldn't hold back, was too excited to be with me—it awoke parts of me I never knew existed.

I look away quickly. I don't know if any of those males will be able to keep me, and I don't want everyone here to see my heart in my eyes. Still I can't resist shooting one more glance in their direction. This time Tarren looks at me and scowls, but I can still see male interest in his eyes. He's worried.

My fear ratchets higher.

King Zander is answering questions, but he gives an impatient flick of his hand and the crowd falls silent again. "Those Zandians willing to volunteer, step forward and be counted."

There's a great shuffling of bodies and beings. Humans shift to the side where I'm standing, Zandians males move toward the makeshift dais where Zander stands.

My mates are among the first to step forward. Master Seke speaks to them, but without the voice amplifier, I can't hear what he's saying.

Lily murmurs, "I heard for the first groups that volunteer, King Zander's going to waive the DNA testing and let them request a choice, to make the whole thing more appealing." She reaches out to touch my freshly pierced earlobe. "So that means you're all set."

I try to school my face to keep it from showing my extreme relief.

From the looks on the faces of all the Zandians, making mating more appealing is not at all necessary. They seem practically bursting to start the mating process immediately, even before any kind of domes or assignments, judging from the hungry looks on their faces.

"Where are the domes going to be?" I peer into the distance, but nothing is visible but debris, all the way to the horizon.

"I'm not sure, but I think some are far from the capital," she explains, "in the areas of the planet that have been overmined."

I feel a pinch of anxiety. What if things go wrong with my mates and I have no friends around to comfort me? No other humans?

But then I catch Jax's thoughtful gaze. He's staring across the plaza at me as if he's deciphering every small emotion bouncing around inside me. As if he plans to alleviate every worry.

"I heard from Thalia there are places on the planet that are still lush and beautiful, with the natural crystals unmined."

I remember Thalia is one of the few Zandian females. She'd been kidnapped by the Finn and held here before Tomis, her warrior, rescued her.

"Too bad we won't get sent there." I try to imagine shimmering crystals, walls and caves of them, crystals sparkling amidst green plants. I don't miss the slaves on the agrifarm, but I do miss working with plants, and the smell of verdant life. My fingers itch to touch soft leaves again. I cross my arms over my chest as a hot breeze attacks me from all sides. I slide my gaze to my friend. "Will you and Rok homestead, too?"

She shrugs. "I don't know. I think he wants to. We'll have to see if King Zander allows it. I know he won't stand for me being mated to other males, though."

I almost laugh out loud at the thought. Her male is as dominant and possessive as they come. It probably takes males who have already bonded or are family, like mine, to make this work.

"Eventually, teams will rebuild the cities as well." Her voice loses some spark as she joins me in searching the horizon. "Although it does seem a monumental task." She sighs. Then her voice brightens. "But think about how exciting it will be, Riya. We have a planet now. It's ours." Her voice is full of pride.

Lily is the one who sold the idea of freedom to the humans on the death pod. She was on it, too, and her mate Rok brought it down with the help of King Zander. I think she's probably also the one who sold the idea to Rok and Zander to engage humans in the Zandian war effort. Otherwise, we'd all be dead. I'm grateful for her influence. Still, I think she's overly idealistic or optimistic to call this planet *ours*.

"It's the Zandian's," I correct her, biting my lip.

"No." Her voice is fierce. She's as much a warrior as her mate when she wants to be. I stare at her. "Riya, you heard him. It's *ours*. All of ours. Zandian and human together. Our shared DNA will mix and rebuild this world into something powerful and strong, stronger than either of our species were alone. They are in charge, yes, but our DNA is half the story. It's ours too. And I, for one, am grateful."

I sure as hell hope she's right. Even if my DNA won't be making any personal contributions.

"My nephew is proof, Riya." She's referring to little prince Zander. Her voice, softer now, is still firm. "He's all of our future, yours, too. Soon you will have a child of your own, more than one, and you will know how amazing it feels to know that you are providing life. Not just for this planet rotation, for a thousand eons, star willing."

My heart swells with untested emotions. As a slave, I was taught that I was inferior, lower, stupid. Good for nothing but breeding to make more slaves. That my human race was annihilated because they were weak, and I was lucky to be alive as a worker. That the future was not mine, and I only existed to serve the superior races on their way to galaxial domination. The idea that me—my DNA, is useful and even powerful? It's a strange new idea, and it frightens me.

But I can't participate the way they need me to. I will eventually be found out as useless for the future. I should disclose the truth now. At least to Lily.

Hell, she may not be able to bear young either. She was a sex slave before Rok rescued her. She may have been altered not to conceive.

But I see my males looking over at me with—oh stars— is it pride? And I can't even bring myself to speak the words out loud. I can't consider the alternative to being their mate. Maybe I could petition to stay on Zandia anyway, devote myself to being a helper in a dome, even if I'm not a mate, but the thought makes me feel dead inside.

Besides, I don't even know if the Zandians would consider that worth the food and air I'd be consuming, or if they would just send me away? I can't risk it.

T*arren*

We're queued up in front of Zander to petition for our homestead and I've lost sight of Riya. My hands curl into fists at my side. Ronan tosses me a curious glance. I know I'm radiating aggression, but I can't dial it back.

There's too much at stake right now. If Zander insists on DNA testing for Riya and matches her with another group, I will *vecking* kill every member of that group with my bare hands. No beings are going to get between us and our mate.

Even if it means defying my king.

Veck.

Could I do that? I'm not sure. I owe everything to King Zander. His fortitude and determination are the reason we won back our planet and have this opportunity to return home.

Still, my need to have Riya by my side eclipses all else.

We step forward. King Zander has taken a seat where he is listening to the petitions of his subjects one by one.

Jax steps forward first and I'm grateful for my cousin's silver tongue. His ability to smooth any situation over. "King Zander, my cousins and I have claimed and pierced our mate. We are ready for your assignment to a homestead." He says it with utter confidence, even though I know he's as worried as the rest of us. That's his gift—presenting things in a way that makes beings fall into his plans.

Zander nods. "Who is your mate?"

Jax clears his throat. "Her name is Riya."

Zander activates his voice amplifier. "Riya."

I scan the crowd of humans, searching for her. She emerges, face pale and pinched. My fists squeeze tighter. I want to do battle for her. Kill any being who's ever frightened her, but I can't comfort her yet. Not until we win this bid for our future.

"Come forward," orders Zander, and she moves as if traveling through a thick mud. Her every step seems to take forever. No, that must be my perception—I want to get this over with faster.

She turns to look over her shoulder at the human, Lily, who gives her a human gesture I don't understand. The thumb of one hand is lifted in the air.

Riya looks back at me and touches her earlobe, as if checking to see if the proof of our claiming is still there. The crystals sparkle in the light, sending a surge of possessive pride through me. I lift my chest.

Ours.

She's ours like no other could ever be.

And no others will ever take her from us.

When she approaches the king, we flank her, Ronan and Jax on either side of her, me behind.

King Zander looks at all of us in that thoughtful way of his. "Riya."

She curtsies. "My lord." Her voice wobbles a little. It's probably her first time meeting the king, which only compounds her stress.

"Have you willingly mated these three males?"

She appears as surprised by the question as we are, but nods without hesitation. "Yes, my lord."

He lets his gaze travel over each of us again. "And you are all willing to serve Zandia through this rehabilitation project? You vow to defend the land, provide your labor toward rebuilding and re-vegetation and remain there for at least five solars, after which the land will belong to you."

"We do, my lord," Jax answers. Ronan and I bow our agreement.

He turns to the warrior beside him. "Do we have Riya's slave data?"

Riya stiffens. I'm not the only one who notices. Jax sends her a speculative look. Ronan catches her hand and squeezes it.

Zander's assistant shakes his head. "I don't have it here, my lord. I can locate it and send it to your data cuff."

Zander waves a dismissive hand. "Send it to her mates when you find it." He turns to Riya. "What purpose did you serve for the Ocretions?"

She swallows audibly. "I worked on an agrifarm, my lord."

Zander's expression brightens. "That will serve your team well. Your skills will be in high demand on the Egantian Mine site. And what were you sentenced to death for?"

Riya shifts on her feet. Her face has gone pale. "I killed a guard, my lord." Her voice cracks.

I squeeze my fists so hard my knuckles pop. I know, without a shadow of a doubt, if Riya killed someone it was because they forced her to. King Zander seems to know this, too, because he shows no shock or disapproval. "In self-defense?"

"Yes, my lord." Her lips barely move.

He lifts his fist in our traditional salute. "You depart immediately. You'll be briefed on the flight. You already know how to construct the dome. Further instructions and expectations will follow. A transport craft is standing by with all your materials and equipment. Please accept my gratitude for helping rebuild Zandia."

Immediately. I suspect we're all surprised, but I'm not sorry. The sooner we get settled with our mate on our homestead, the better. I want everything settled and sure.

My cousins and I return the salute and Riya curtsies, although I suspect Ronan's holding her up because her knees appear wobbly.

As we walk away, my whole body fills with exultation. *Yes*. We asked for her, and by the stars, she is here. An uncharacteristic smile stretches my face, pinching my healing wound. I assume Ronan also wears his goofy grin, but I only have eyes for Riya.

She looks terrified and relieved, at once. Well, that's understandable. This is something entirely new for all of us. Although our mating together was phenomenal, forging a lifelong bond is something we will all learn together.

When we reach the edge of the gathering, we stop, and I hold out a hand for Riya. She doesn't take it, though. She bites her lip. "So what do we do now?" Her voice is low, and despite the obvious joy that flashed on her face when Zander thanks us, she seems scared.

Ronan lifts their twined hands and kisses the back of hers. "Well, I suggest that all four of us mate right here in front of everyone, just to prove we're a team. You know how that kind of thing always brings a crowd together."

Her lips part and brows come down, like she's not sure if he's serious. Ronan laughs. "I'm teasing you, Riya. Trying to make you smile."

"You idiot," I snap, trying not to punch him in the jaw. His joke is as stupid as it is inappropriate. Our mate is scared and requires reassurance. "Riya..."

But then she giggles, the relief on her face is evident. "Very funny."

I turn away. "Let's go," I snap. Part of me is grateful Ronan, always the light-hearted one, made our mate smile in the midst of her unease. I don't want to be jealous, because that is simply not a useful emotion. But part of me seethes as she continues to grip his hand more tightly when we enter the transport craft.

"Do you have your things prepared? Ours are ready to go, including supplies for the homestead." Jax touches her arm, and she nods, swallowing hard.

"The few things I have," she replies with a short nod, staring out the window, before looking back at us. "I don't come with a large inventory... of items. Just a few articles of clothing."

Ronan gives her that smile of his, the one that melts hearts around the galaxy. "All we care about is you," he says, honestly. "We will make what we need on our homestead. Together."

She twirls a lock of her dark hair around one finger, still nervous. "I suppose that's true."

I want to reassure her, but *veck* if I know what home-steading will be like. All I know is how proud I am that she's our mate.

4

Tarren

N ow that we're all seated close to each other, I breathe in her scent: amazing. A sort of light, floral aroma, something that seems like it would shimmer if it were a color. And underneath that, something musky and pleasant and... aroused? I lean in a little bit to see if I'm right. *Veck*, she is aroused. I hold back the urge to grab her and take her right there. First we need to get to our homestead.

"Have you been told anything about the planet?" I'm curious to see what kind of information she's been given; how useful she'll be from the start.

She blinks, and her eyes—so wide and pretty, make me get hard. "When we were on the training pod, we had some meetings together to learn about Zandian history, biology, and agriculture. Natural resources. Nothing of what we'd do here. Or what would be expected of us." Color tinges her cheeks.

Is she thinking about what we expect of her... sexually?

Because I sure as hell am.

I fight back a triumphant grin. This little female might be nervous, and has a traumatic past, but she still wants us. This much I can tell.

"And what are your expectations of what your role will be?"

"Well, for me." She takes a breath. "I imagine I'll prepare my own meals since you three don't eat much. I'll keep our domicile orderly and assist all three of you with tasks as appropriate re-vegetating the land. I'm going to create and tend our garden and be the caretaker for any animals. Will we have domestic beasts?"

I stare at her in surprise. "What for?"

She flushes. "To eat. On the agrifarm we kept many beasts that provided food products."

I nod. "That sounds like a wonderful idea. I'll see if we can catch some beasts for you to domesticate."

Her eyes widen. "Well," she stammers. "I-I don't know if I know how to domesticate animals that weren't born that way, but," she swallows and nods. "I'm sure we'll figure it out."

Damn, our mate is brave.

"I personally plan to cultivate my knowledge of local and imported herbs and botanicals to help create new medicines for humans and Zandians. And of course... young. If, er, when we have young, I'll take care of them." She avoids my eye and I notice her fingers are closed in a fist.

I wonder if she's scared of the birthing process. I saw a hologram—and *veck*, it looked gory, but with Dr. Daneth and the females who know a lot about this, I'm sure it will all be as safe as possible.

Her face lightens. "I know a lot about plants and botanical propagation. I'm confident I can make the best garden you've ever seen and come up with landscape improvement plans we can share with all of the teams. Her voice is fervent, and it does something strange to my insides. They rearrange to make room for the warmth in my chest.

Jax touches her arm. His voice is low and calm, like he always seems to be. "It will be new for all of us. We'll figure it out together." He smiles at her.

The muscles in her face soften. "Yes. Thank you."

I stare out the window as our assigned homestead site comes into view.

It's... totally barren. We're supposed to erect our dome on a pile of mine tailings and broken boulders.

"Is that... it?" Riya asks. My chest feels like it just caved in. How are we supposed to make our mate happy in this stark, ugly place?

And what happened to the planet of my youth? It makes me want to demolish the Finn all over again. They ruined our beautiful planet.

Ronan curses. "Is it too late to request an assignment in the capital?"

Even Jax appears deflated.

"Well," Riya says, and I'm shocked to see her smiling. "We're intended to improve it, right? So we can't view it for what it is now. Imagine what we can do with it."

"What?" Ronan asks doubtfully.

She grins. "Anything we want."

My heart tumbles in my chest. Our sweet female is so *vecking* brave. So strong and willing. Of course she's probably lived in worse conditions than this. The Ocretions raped her home planet Earth of its resources until it became uninhabitable. They've over-mined and over-produced on every planet they've invaded. Her agrifarm probably didn't look like much.

The craft lands and I insist on lifting her out, mainly because I need to touch her. To thank her for her optimism.

The warrior who brought us helps us unload the supplies and departs, leaving us with no means of leaving our new homestead.

We'd better hope to the Zandian star we're able to figure out how to homestead here, because we have nowhere else to go.

I glance at the sky. The Zandian sun will set in a few hours and we have to get the dome built before nightfall or our mate will sleep in a tent, something I'm not willing to ask of her.

"Let's get to work," I mutter. "Riya, stay close while we get the dome built."

Jax and Ronan fall in beside me as we fit together beams and snap together the high-tech materials to build our dome. Riya watches, making herself useful by handing us parts or tools.

I don't know about Jax and Ronan, but having her watch makes it hard for me to concentrate. Especially the way she gazes up under those long lashes at my chest and arms, as if she's fascinated by my muscles.

We finish just before sundown. The dome shines silver against the sky. The interior has been designed with controlled humidity and temperature. The exterior is strong to protect against storms, wild beasts, and any other threats.

It's set up to utilize the sun and wind for energy production, but we won't have water until we tap the well next planet rotation. For now, we have enough in the tank to get by.

"Come in and look around." I am proud to show the dome to her. Our home—complete only with her. It's magnificent.

R *iya*

I saw the domes they were putting up in the capital but seeing the males—my mates—put ours up so efficiently was breathtaking. The structure itself is vast, the top criss-crossed with silver beams and dotted with glass. The area outside the dome is rough, that's for sure, but I saw a stream nearby when we landed, so I'm confident I can get something to grow on it. It will look completely different in a few solar cycles once the vegetation returns.

The inside is luxurious, at least compared to what I'm used to. There's a pantry for food storage and preparation, and an eating section with a table and chairs. A storage room for clothing, tools, and weapons. A washroom equipped with an automated washtube like they had in the palatial pod. A common area for relaxation, with hover-chairs and tables. And... the sleeping chamber. Like my mate's chamber in the palatial pod, there's one large hoverdisk composed of three smaller ones. There are smaller hoverseats along the wall, for relaxation, possibly. The hoverdisk is outfitted with soft fabrics and a flowing canopy.

"I never dreamed I'd have a home of my own," I admit to my mates, who trail me through the dome, watching my every reaction as I take it all in. "As an agrifarm slave, I slept on the floor in a tent with the other slaves. We weren't allowed privacy or the right to own anything." I touch the finely woven fabric on the hoverdisk.

But I'm getting soft. I shouldn't get used to this. I can't. It may not be mine for long. Am I foolish enough to think I'll get to stay here for the five years until it becomes ours? My mates will figure out I'm not a breeder soon enough and they'll petition for a new one.

"Everything here is yours, now, Riya." Tarren's voice is hard.

Tears spring to my eyes at his declaration and alarm flickers over Tarren's face. I have to remember Zandians don't understand human emotions. At least that's what I've heard. They're both mystified by the complexity of our emotions, and also influenced by them—becoming more emotional themselves when they bond with us.

"I'm sorry." I wipe my cheeks rapidly.

Tarren turns away, but I think I see something flash in his eyes. He's so guarded, and I feel the urge to break down his defenses and find out what he's like inside, when he's not putting up his rough exterior.

After I tour our new home, I return outside, where the crates of equipment stand under the setting sun. The warriors follow me, as if my every reaction fascinates them. "What's in here?"

"I imagine that's whatever they think we need to homestead. Shall we see?" Jax asks. He pries open the lid of one crate and peers inside.

"Here is your stockpile of seeds," Tarren calls out in his gruff voice, opening several palettes of silvery boxes. "And tools."

My breath catches, and I eagerly bend down to open the air-tight latches on the first box. On my training holo on the transport craft, I received an overview of what seeds we'd receive, what needed to be planted for sure, and what was optional, based on our personal team needs and desires. We were told we'd receive help if we needed it, but with my background, I'm confident.

"Wheat," I exclaim at the first packet. "Carrots, tomatoes, beans, onions." I go through packet after packet. "Strawberries, potatoes, spinach, chard." There are also boxes of herbs, vitamins, and fertilizers.

"This must be worth a fortune." My voice is full of awe. "How did King Zander obtain this?" I gesture at the riches in front of me. Earth foods are still prized, even if Earth is long gone. Their legacy, apart from human slaves, was our superior foodstuffs.

"King Zander has been purchasing heirloom seeds since he mated his human," Jax tells me. I remember all the lush food-bearing plants I'd seen in the palatial pod. Ronan had told me Lamira planted them. She was previously an agri-farm slave like me. "Our crystals are highly prized, and we are able to get vast amounts of things in exchange for even small amounts of them." He holds out one fist. "A crystal that could fit into my hand probably provided the seeds and paid for the materials for all of the domes."

"Some of these things I've never tasted," I admit to them.

"No?" Tarren looks surprised. "Why not?"

I shrug. "Even though we were responsible for growing it, slaves were harshly punished for eating even a mouthful of food that was grown for Ocretions."

My stomach twists remembering my life before the Zandians rescued us. Thank the stars it is different now. These seeds, these plants in the making, these will be mine. I can taste them. I feel such joy at the idea that I jump up and throw my arms around Tarren. His body stiffens but he clasps me, a second later.

Ronan scowls. "Riya, from now forward, you'll eat whatever you want. In fact, I'll make it my personal goal to feed you every single one of these foods every planet rotation, until you beg me to stop." He looks at a packet. "This one. Corn. You shall have corn three times a planet rotation if you wish. Seven times." He laughs.

I giggle and snatch the packet out of his hand. "I think once a week for corn is plenty." The Zandians don't understand human eating. To them, it's as strange as their crystal sustenance is to me. "But I have plans to extract the syrup from the corn kernels and experiment—turn it into an oily fuel. I think it could possibly be useful, although I'm not sure just how, yet." So many ideas swirl in my mind.

Ronan cocks his head. "Fuel from this?" He looks at the picture, surprise etched into his expression. "It sounds impossible. But I trust you. Soon we will have the best homestead on the planet and I will tell beings our mate is a miracle worker."

The vast open space fills me with a giddy joy. "This is incredible." I spin around. "I think the wheat should go in that field, there, to take advantage of the sun. And strawberries there, but beneath the peas and beans, because they will do well as ground shrubs. I think the tomatoes and chard should go—" I break off. "Unless you want them elsewhere?" I hesitate.

Surprise flits over Jax's face. "You will decide what to plant, where." He points to the land. "And we will plow it for you and do the work to make it so."

I am taken aback. "I will tell you?"

"How else will we know where to plant them?" He looks at me. "We trust your judgement. You will know more about this than I."

"But I thought you were going to give me orders."

His mouth quirks up. "I'm sure I'll give you plenty of

orders, but most of them will be in our chamber, little human. You're not a slave any longer, Riya. You're our mate."

Ronan comes up and snakes his arm around my waist, pulling my back against his front. "I have a few orders I'd like to give right now." The dark suggestion in his voice has my feminine parts flaring to life. My freshly pierced nipples, which are slightly sore now that the analgesic spray has worn off, bead up.

I'm here with three handsome powerful males who expect to bed me again. *Soon.* Very soon, judging by the way they keep touching me, looking at me with those hungry eyes. Even Tarren, the gruffest of my mates, wants me... badly.

R onan

"I nside, female." I don't release Riya, but propel her toward the dome, keeping her delectable ass pressed against the front of my body.

I don't know about my cousins, but I can't wait any longer to claim our mate again. I've never felt so grateful for another being in my life.

Her upbeat attitude is about the only thing that saved mine from going straight to my boots when I saw our homestead site. But she's right. With her knowledge of agriculture, we'll be able to transform this place into something beautiful again.

I'm so damn grateful for her. She's already so much more than I ever imagined we'd find in a mate. And I don't mind sharing her at all. In fact, it makes it easier because I wouldn't know how in the *veck* to keep a female satisfied. But I'm confident between the three of us, we'll figure it out.

Riya allows me to maneuver her inside, the incredible scent of her arousal making my dick turn harder than Zandian crystal.

My cousins are right behind me. I think I hear Tarren growling in anticipation. I take her to our sleeping chamber and release her.

"Take off your clothing," I order.

She casts a nervous look at the three of us looming before her but doesn't move to comply.

"I think she prefers to have it done for her," Jax says mildly, strolling easily forward. He grips her tunic and pulls it over her head.

Her breasts bounce free and this time I'm sure Tarren's growling. It rumbles right in harmony with my groan.

Jax walks around behind Riya and cups her breasts. "She'll learn soon enough to obey us." He pinches both her nipples, gently tugging on the new studs decorating her nipples.

She gasps, but it's not fear I read on her face, it's a lust equal—I hope—to ours. Her cheeks flush with color, her pupils are wide and black, darkening the gold of her eyes.

"Little mates who are slow to submit get punished," Jax murmurs, his lips right at her ear. He bites the place where her neck meets shoulder.

She shivers, but I don't think it's from fear.

"Boots off. Quickly now or Ronan will get the strap from that box Dr. Daneth gave us."

She jumps to comply, looking adorable as she hops on one foot and pulls off the boots that make her legs look so *vecking* sexy.

Jax hooks his thumbs in the waistband of her leggings and slides them, along with her panties, to the floor. She steps out of them, twisting her hands in front of her body. Jax catches her hands and places them behind her head. "Let my cousins look at you, beautiful. You're the sweetest thing we've seen in our lives."

I nod my agreement, giving my cock a rough squeeze through my pants as I advance. "Spread your legs, sweet girl," I command. As soon as she does, I cup her mons, swallowing her gasp with my mouth. I suck her lower lip, sweep my tongue into her mouth. I want to devour our pretty mate.

Her pussy leaks honey onto my fingers, flesh growing plumper with each stroke. She's so damn responsive—it nearly undoes me.

"This pussy," I growl when I end the kiss. She stares up at me with surprise. "Must be the most perfect pussy on the entire planet." I screw one finger into her and she almost falls forward, attempting to recover her hands from Jax. He keeps her captive though, caging her hands in one of his as he toys with her breasts with the other. Tarren watches from the hoverdisk. He's removed his clothes and washed up, and he strokes his cock now.

"Where do you want my cock, Riya?" I ask her, adding a second finger and *vecking* her with them.

She gasps and squirms, eyes going glassy.

"Do you want it here? In your pussy?"

"Y-yes," she gasps, and I kiss her again.

Jax releases her and I usher her over to the hoverdisk, where I fold her torso down onto the mattress. Her ass is so pretty, just waiting to be turned pink again, so I slap it, hard.

She squeaks but doesn't stray from her position. I slap her again and again until her skin turns a beautiful shade of pink. Then I release my cock and stroke the head over her slit.

My eyes roll back in my head when I enter her, and I groan. I ease in, giving her time to adjust to my size. My thighs shake from the effort of holding back, but I distract myself by running my palms up and down her sides, down the elegant slope of her back. When she arches and pushes back to take me deeper, I bark out a curse. Holding back is no longer an option. I grip her hips and pull back, then fill her with every inch of me.

She cries out, but it has a wanton quality to it, so I go on. Every time I plow deep, she makes little mewls of pleasure until all I can hear are her cries, my grunts, and the slap of flesh between us. Jax crawls over on the hoverdisk and lifts her head with her hair, mating their mouths. Tarren reaches his fingers under her hips, rubbing the place that makes her go wild.

She starts to tighten around me and I lose control. My balls tighten, thighs shake. I pound into her two, three more times, then bury myself deep and come.

"Come, Riya," Tarren commands, but it's not necessary. Our little mate is already coming like a meteor. Her muscles squeeze and milk my cock of every last drop of cum.

"That's it, sweet mate," I croon, draping my torso over hers, utterly replete.

R *iya*

. . .

I continue to be amazed that sex with my mates hasn't brought up any thoughts of violation or the abuse I suffered before. Not even a hint of it. It's like my body knows its owners, responds to their touch like I was made only for them.

I hardly notice as Ronan eases out of me and Tarren sits beside me on the hoverdisk. Some being rubs my back. Another massages my scalp. Bliss still courses through me, thick and warm.

Tarren brings me back to reality when he lifts me and puts me over his and Jax's laps.

I squeak in dismay, at first thinking they're going to spank me again. But Tarren has another idea entirely. "Spread your thighs," he tells me, "and loosen your bottom cheeks. I am going to insert a training device into your back hole to spread you out. That way you will be able to accept Jax's member and we can both share you at once."

I can feel how hard and long Jax is beneath my thighs, and I clench up automatically. There is no way he'll fit into me that way without a lot of pain.

"Relax," Tarren soothes me, his voice softer than I've ever heard it. "We'll take care of you. You can trust us."

"Dr. Daneth assured me," Ronan adds, reaching out to stroke my thigh, "With training you'll be able to take us in the ass, quite well. And that you'll enjoy it." He gives me a soft spank and laughs. "You will see."

I'm dubious, but I also am fascinated, and my body thrums with desire. I've heard other humans talk about how good this feels, and Mother Earth, I'm eager to find out. The plug is coated with some kind of lubricant, and when Tarren pushes it against my body, I relax my muscles to allow entrance.

"That's it," encourages Jax. "Just let him push it in all the way. Don't fight it. If you push back against it, it will go in more easily."

"It hurts," I whimper, as a burning pain arises at the widest part of the plug.

"Just for a minute," agrees Jax, stroking my back and thighs. "Once it's in entirely, the pain will cease. I promise."

Tarren slides one hand underneath my belly and presses his fingers up into me with his other hand while he presses the plug again to my entrance.

As he strokes me from below, I relax, and then he pushes the plug in again. This time I'm ready, and his fingers on my clit are driving me insane.

"Good girl, legs nice and wide, muscles loose," encourages Jax, as Tarren presses the device further into me, and it seats itself.

Jax brushes my clit. "You see?" he says. "The pain is gone now, yes?"

I nod. "Yes." It feels odd, though, foreign.

Tarren gives me a little slap across the buttocks. "It's not as large as Jax's cock will be, but it's enough to open you up for him."

Flutters surge in my stomach at this. Something even bigger?

"And it will feel even tighter," Tarren says calmly, "because you'll have my cock inside you as well. But first we'll get you ready."

He lies me down on the hoverdisk, spreads my legs, and kneels beside me. He leans down and puts his mouth to my nipple and I cry out, instant desire surging. It feels amazing, and when Jax puts his head between my thighs to lick my clit, it ratchets my need higher. The constant flicking at my clit and nipples is phenomenal, and soon I'm writhing as I try to push my body up to their mouths.

"Look at her clit," Jax says in amazement. "So swollen."

"She's even wetter than before," Tarren adds. "I think she's ready for us to take her."

He leans over me to look into my eyes. "Riya, do you want Jax to put his cock into your ass?"

I can barely breathe, and the words come immediately. "Yes, I want it."

Jax gets up and sits back, his thighs partly spread.

"Come on." Tarren sits on the edge himself and pulls me closer. "Let's take out that plug now so Jax can replace it with his cock."

"Yes, please, please," I murmur. I don't even care if it hurts. If his cock in my ass means an orgasm, he can put it there as often as he wants.

Tarren picks me up as easily as if I were made of air. "When I lower you down, keep your ass cheeks loose," he says. "I'll let you stand on the floor and lower yourself onto Jax's cock. If you go slowly, it won't hurt."

"Yes," I whisper, and he rubs more lubricant around my tight hole.

"Now," he tells me, setting me onto Jax's lap and allowing me to stand, my thighs parted, my ass cleft pressing down against Jax's hard, straining cock. "Wiggle until you feel him at the very entrance, then lower down."

Jax takes my hips into his hands. "Like this, Riya."

At first, it feels like the plug, but as he presses me downward, his cock pressing further into my body, his greater width makes it a much tighter fit.

"Oh," I gasp, as the pain increases.

"Ease up," suggests Tarren, and bends over to lick my nipples. "Riya, you look so vecking amazing like this, your pussy wet for us to veck, so obedient, sinking down onto Jax's cock. You're the hottest being in the galaxy right now."

I stand back up to relieve the burn, and Jax's strong hands hold my hips, and now Tarren has his hands on my shoulders, providing a firm pressure while he sucks my nipples.

Jax reaches around and strokes my clit, and soon enough I'm pushing into his fingers, all discomfort forgotten in the quest for pleasure.

"The sooner you take my entire length, the sooner you will get accustomed to me," Jax urges, and presses my hips downward.

This time the lubrication and my arousal do the trick, and I find my body opening up, little by little, to accept his thick, hard cock. I gasp when I find myself on his thighs, his entire length inside me.

"The first time is the worst," Jax soothes me, pressing his lips to my shoulder. "It will be easier next time, Riya."

Even as he speaks, having him inside me feels good. Really good. He begins to move, his strong arms controlling me effortlessly on his cock. After a few minutes, he shifts me faster, harder, and a tingling need grows inside of me, somewhere deep, mysterious.

"Oh, it feels so good," I cry, breathless.

Tarren groans. "Now it's time for me, Riya."

Jax uses his hands on my hips to stand me up, his cock releasing from my ass with a pop, and hands me over to Tarren, who sits down and pulls me to straddle him. "You're going to ride my cock, Riya," he mutters, and it's only a second later before he impales me onto his member. He's even longer and thicker than Jax, and I'm relieved that he's the one in my pussy. And Mother Earth, does it feel good.

He's pressing on all the parts of me that I like to stroke; even my clit rubs against him where our bodies mate.

"Ride, Riya," he orders.

So I do. The minute I start, the rhythm makes itself known to me, and I find that I can control the depth and places he rubs me. He grabs my nipples and squeezes, twists them in his fingers, uses them as handles. It's fantastic, and I pant, working my thighs to bounce harder.

I barely notice Jax behind me, and when Tarren stops me from moving for a minute so Jax can spread my ass cheeks and apply more lubricant, I obediently loosen my muscles and tip up my hips so Jax can enter my ass more easily.

At first it burns when Jax's cock enters my ass, but within seconds it's back to the bliss. I can't tell where my body ends and theirs begin; all I know is that with two huge Zandian cocks in my ass and pussy, I'm going to die from pleasure. Jax pumps me hard from behind, and the force of his movements push me up and down on Tarren's cock. Tarren assists by gripping my hips and adjusting me. I can smell Tarren's body when I ride him, musky and like forest, and my own sex wafting up to me every time Jax pumps. I'm so wet I can hear my pussy making little squelching sounds on Tarren's cock, and Jax's groans each time he *vecks* me harder.

"Are you close?" Tarren grunts.

"Yes," I whisper.

"Yes," roars Jax.

"Riya, you may come once both of us come," Tarren orders.

Jax stiffens and I feel his cock shoot hot fluid into me. At the same time, Tarren jerks in my pussy, and the feeling of being so full sets me off. I scream out my pleasure, falling into the most exquisite orgasm of my life. My whole body is full of glittering light and joy.

When I awake, I'm on the hoverdisk in Tarren's arms, with a soft cover over me. Jax lies beside us, his hand on top of my thigh through the blanket, and Ronan is on the other side, his hand on my ankle. I hold my breath, because Tarren's stroking my hair, a gesture so tender—especially coming from him—that I don't want to ruin the moment.

But they all notice immediately. "Riya," Tarren says, his voice gruff. "How are you feeling?"

I shift experimentally. "I'm fine." I flush. "Good."

My pussy and bottom feel used, but in a good way. The residual tinge feels nice, a reminder of what happened.

"You are ours," Ronan says, his voice confident and tender. "Truly ours."

"For always," Jax adds, squeezing my thigh.

Tarren just grunts, but he holds me tighter in his arms, and that act is so tender that tears come to my eyes.

"Are you sad?" Ronan peers at me, blinking, muscles tense—as if he's ready to do battle.

"No." I moisten my lips with my tongue. "Happy," I croak. For the first time in my life, I think I'm truly happy.

He growls, and the pleased look on his face is beyond joy. And as all four of us drift into sleep, Tarren keeps me in his arms. I've never slept better, or more soundly.

5

Ronan

I awake early, when the gray dawn is just starting to turn pink and gold. My cousins are deep in slumber. Riya is dreaming still, her lashes fluttering on her cheeks, entangled in Tarren's limbs. I assume we'll figure out over time how to take turns being the one to hold her as she falls asleep.

Heading out of the dome, I stand tall, enjoying the morning alone, as I survey our land. A feeling of pride suffuses me, and a sense of duty. I'm not as strong or tall as Tarren or Jax, and I'm not the most handsome Zandian in the universe, so I need to work twice as hard to prove myself. I leave the dome and take a deep breath of air—fresh Zandian air, unpolluted now. I start organizing crates of equipment into piles—tools, foodstuffs, and clothing.

As I wipe sweat from my brow, I sense her behind me. I turn in an instant and can't resist smiling at her like an idiot, and I nearly trip in my haste to embrace her.

RENEE ROSE & REBEL WEST

"Good morning." I pull her to me, awkward at first. But she enters my arms willingly and presses her cheek to my chest.

"Hi." She seems shy, a pink flush to her cheeks.

"How are you?" I examine her face. "It's a big change, coming here, to all of this. With us." I wave my hand.

"I'm content." She meets my eyes. "Thank you."

This makes me exuberant. "I'm just sorry we all fell asleep last rotation without getting the chance to pleasure you again." I want to give her so many orgasms, bring that look of sated joy to her face a million times, that she never needs to think again about the Ocretians. The instinct to protect her from pain surprises me with its ferocity.

"I do enjoy the pleasure." She flushes harder, but smiles.

"And that's just the start," I tease her, relief and joy filling me. "We have so much more planned for your sweet body. And of course," I hasten to add, not wanting her to think we only care about vecking her, "our lives together."

Her eyes widen, and at first I think she's scared, but then I scent her arousal.

"I can't wait," she says, and winds her fingers into mine. Her smile is wide and trusting, and she seems almost surprised at her own joy. "This is so unexpected," she discloses, squeezing my hand.

Lust kicks through me and I want to mate her again, but I assume she may need time to rejuvenate first. I clear my throat. "Do you want to tell me where to till the soil for seeds? We can get an early start."

"Yes." She nods. "I want our homestead to be the best one, the one that shows all the others how to do it."

Her voice rings out strong, and I smile. I *vecking* love seeing this competitive side of her. It matches well with ours. "We need to lead the way in new innovations. I've already been thinking..." she trails off and continues. "On the agrifarm, I experimented with a new recipe for fertilizer using a different ratio of nitrogen, to better *fix* it —you know that *fixing* means locking it down for less nitrogen loss, right? I also added more Vitamin B from the standard. And it resulted in faster growth and more fruit on the tomato vines. I'd like to try that here."

"Of course." I nod. "I admit that your talk of nitrogen means as little to me as an Ocretian saying *blah blah blah*,"— and I make a face at her and draw out the syllables as if I'm drooling—"but I trust your judgement."

Jax said Riya was smart. I think she's brilliant. Human slaves don't learn to decipher or write with instruments. They are kept from communication devices that would give them knowledge. So the fact that she knows so much stuns me.

I hope we can help her build her confidence—mates do that, I think, for each other.

She laughs, a gorgeous sound, like a bird in flight, and her whole face glows. "That's *exactly* how they sound." She squeezes my fingers.

I take a risk. "*Blah blah blah,* Riya, show me where to *blah blah blah* the soil," I rumble at her, crossing my eyes and holding up my fingers like fangs, even though Ocretians don't have fangs. I sense that mocking them is something she needs right now, and I want to give her whatever she desires.

She laughs again and puts a hand to her mouth. "Oh, Mother Earth, this is hilarious." She looks around as if someone might be watching, then laughs at that, too. "I love that we have our own place. And it's safe." She says the word as if it's a treasure.

I squeeze her to me. "Yes. As safe as we can make it. The only dangers here are our own flaws, Riya. And, of course, the wild beasts that live near the forests. They can be fierce, so we must avoid them. But there are no slave masters here. We own our destiny, now."

Together we look across the barren land, past the silvery edges of the dome shimmering in the Zandian sun.

"Did I see water when we landed? Is there a stream here?" she asks. "Show me?"

So I do. I take her hand, although it's not necessary—she is nimble and quick—but I enjoy the warmth of her small, delicate fingers in mine. When we reach the hill, a short walk from our home, she gasps.

"But it's so pretty." She blinks hard. "It's gorgeous. Can we drink it? Swim in it? Use it for irrigation?"

"Anything we want." I want to hear her laugh again, so I decide to make another joke. I lower my voice. "But we should probably not use it as a toilet, because this is the top of the spring, and all water flows downhill to our pumping system. And Jax's eliminations could ruin the filtration system."

She laughs again until she snorts, and then we're both laughing, and suddenly, without even realizing how it happened, we're lying together in a delicate patch of purple flowers growing beside the stream.

She reaches out to touch my face, and I wait, holding my breath. Letting her make the first move, even though I'm aching to dominate her, take her, make her mine, again and again. "Your skin is so warm." Her voice is full of wonder. Her fingers are doing things to me, and I'm already so *vecking* hard that it's painful.

"Your horns." She reaches up to stroke them with both hands.

I groan as they stiffen with need. "Riya..."

"They turn you on?" She gasps, and then looks at me. "Like your cock. Do you like it when I do... this?" And she gets to her knees and leans over me. At first, I smell the floral scent of her hair, and the musk of her body, and then I forget my entire *vecking* existence as she closes her little lips around my left horn and sucks, experimentally.

"Riya," I groan, my cock twitching, desire rising. "When you do that..."

"This?" She asks with mock innocence that makes me want to spank her. She tongues the other horn. "Does it feel like I'm licking your cock, Ronan?"

She reaches down to stroke me through my pants, teasing the hard outline with her palm, tracing it with her fingers. "Would it feel like you have two mouths on you if I suck here and rub there?" Her hand is busy now, stroking up and down, and *veck*, my cock is about to burst through the cloth. I reach down to release my aching flesh, and she grasps it, stroking firmly, and I shudder.

"Suck my horns harder," I order her, "and keep stroking like that." Yeah, like she's not the one totally in control for the moment, and I don't even care. It feels so good that all I want to do is get lost in this sea of pleasure.

She giggles. "Yes, Master," she whispers, all obedience, and my cock shoots out harder to hear that word on her lips. Then she puts her mouth back to my body and does what I commanded, like it's the only thing in the world that brings her pleasure. Her little moans and sighs make me more aroused until I can't take it anymore.

"On your back," I order roughly, and flip her over. I spread her thighs with one leg and press myself to her. At the same time, I pull her arms over her head and pin her wrists with one hand, while I play with her pierced nipple with the other, through her shirt.

She squeals, and her eyes go dark with desire. She squirms in my grasp, trying to free her wrists. But I can see and smell her arousal, so I hold her down harder, and suck her nipple through the thin fabric until it's taut and hard, outlined by wet silk, and she trembles under my touch.

"Ronan," she begs, her voice hoarse and wild. "Please, fuck me. Please."

She uses the Ocretion word for *veck*, which annoys me. I want to teach her our language, have her only speak in our tongue. "*Master*," I remind her, and slap her thigh, not hard, but a firm spank. Her moan of pleasure lets me know it was the right call, so I do it again, and again until she bucks her hips up at me, panting, eyes glassy.

"Master," she whispers, and her eyes flicker shut, her eyelashes black on her pale cheeks.

"Keep one hand there above your head," I order her, and gently tug down her leggings, exposing her naked pussy. "Spread your thighs for me, Riya. And reach down with the other hand and spread your pussy lips wide open. As wide as you can. Show me what's mine. I'm going to make you do it later for the others, as well, so practice now. Get it right or I'll spank you until you do."

Veck. My dirty command makes her so wet I can see the juices flow.

"No..." she murmurs, and tosses her head from side to side, fisting her hair with her hand.

"I warned you," I growl, and pull her to one side. As I spank her ass hard, one cheek, then the other, I say, "You. Will. Do. As. I. Command."

I check to make sure she's not genuinely afraid, but I

don't think she is because she cries, "Oh! Yes, Master, I will." Her nipples are hard pebbles under her shirt now.

I lay her back down on the flowers and bend over to swipe my tongue up the skin on her belly. I need more immediately, so I dip my head between her legs to lick at the honey there.

She cries out something unintelligible and I warn her, "Don't come yet." I can't wait another second, so I press my cock to the warmth between her thighs. "I'm going to take you hard," I say.

"Yes, yes," she moans, reaching up to grab my horns. Then she gives me the most wicked smile and whispers, "Later on, if you want, I'll lick your horns and your cock until you explode in my mouth."

"*Veck*," I roar, and drive into her, filling her as deeply as I can. She wraps her legs around mine and meets me thrust for thrust, and soon we both come together in a cry of exultation.

We lie there panting until our breathing comes back to normal, with her resting on my chest. I stroke her shoulder and murmur, suddenly worried, "Was it too rough? I don't want to hurt you."

She smiles, her eyes large and wild still from our passion, and kisses my neck. "It just felt good, no pain at all. I think maybe Zandian sperm has healing properties." Her smile falters, as if the topic of sperm concerns her.

I try to bring back the smiles. "If you want, the four of us can start a side business selling our sperm. You get some pretty glass vials, and we'll look at your naked body and jerk off into them every planet rotation. We can probably get a few gallons by the end of this week, easy. We'll label it as a health enhancer and bring it to all the domes."

I study her. Too much? Not everyone likes my sense of

humor. Females, especially, usually prize a male for his strength and prowess on the battlefield, not his ability to make jokes. *Veck.* I hope I haven't ruined—

But she smiles, her chest heaving on mine, her nipples rubbing my skin, sending happiness and relief coursing through my veins. "Sure, if you ever run out of crystals, it can be the new Zandian export. Good for any ailment."

A booming laugh leaves my lips before I can hold it in. I've never had a female be such a fun companion. And I think she needs this too. So as we bathe in the stream, I make more jokes about water purity, and she holds my hand all the way back to the dome.

6

Riya

"You're lying to me." I teasingly poke Jax's chest, as we traverse our Northern-most field, the one I've devoted to my more delicate herbs. It's more like a large garden than a vast terrace, but I have goals.

"I swear I tell the truth." Jax puts a hand to his chest and gives me a smile, the one that melts me. "It's been nearly two lunar cycles already, Riya. You just haven't noticed the passing of time because we keep you so... busy." He winks, and I flush.

"So busy I'm out here late this planet rotation," I retort, "and you're lucky I can even still walk." I give him a mock scowl. But I wind my fingers around his impressive tricep—as far as I can, anyway. My touch tells a different story from my stern look, a tale of remembered passion and all of our cries of pleasure, over and over last night.

"Oh, you can?" He tilts his head. "I must not have done my job properly, then." He tsks disapprovingly. "If your pussy isn't completely devastated by morning, I consider us to have failed our task as mates."

I roll my eyes, because the three of them are so overprotective that it's not even funny. Yes, they *veck* me until I'm hoarse with pleasure, until I can't take another second of it... and then they lavish me with affection and praise, massage my limbs and my feet, bring me honeyed water to drink, until I am fully replenished. If they spank me, which they often do, until I'm pink and begging, they follow it up with orgasms enough to drive any pain from my body, leaving me so sated that I sleep like a stone at midnight, in a dark garden, and awake refreshed to attack the planet rotation with vigor.

"Oh, no. Oh..." I bite my lip hard enough to hurt, all of my lazy leftover bliss snapped, like a twig in a storm.

"What's wrong?" Jax frowns and steps closer, scanning the area around us, and puts a hand onto my shoulder. "Riya?"

"It's my calendula." I fight to keep tears out of my eyes. It's stupid, but I'm trying so damn hard to grow things out here. Trying so hard to prove my worth to my mates beyond a breeder. "It all died... again."

I pull away from his grasp and bend down, as if touching the withered brown wisps will change their fate. "This is the third location I've tried, and now I've wasted more seeds." I dig down to check for the fat white grubs that sometime infiltrate the soil and press the leaves in my fingers to examine them for the silvery trails of caterpillar larva, but all I see is dead brown matter.

"I can't figure it out." My chest tightens, and I get to my feet, dizzy for a second. "I need to figure it out."

Jax frowns and examines my face, steps closer. "Riya, our planting is doing well," he counters. "When I communicated your progress this week to King Zander, he said that you're ahead of all of the other domes." he smiles and adds, "Not that it is a competition. We are all in this together."

"Oh, I know that." I bite my lip and nod, forcing a smile to my lips. "I just want to make you proud." *Because I won't be providing you babies.* Every planet rotation that goes on without me telling them feels like a bigger and bigger lie.

"You already do." He touches my chin. "Not just proud, but happy, Riya. For the first time, I—all of us—have the chance to learn what it's like to *live* life, not just fight for a future chance to live one. Do you know how incredible that is?" He slides his hand up to cup my cheek, still looking at me.

His eyes, so dark, have multiple reflections of the Zandian sun, making them glow. A beam of light accentuates his sharp cheekbone, setting his striking good looks into profile. I catch my breath and put my hand on top of his, a surge of emotion taking me by surprise.

"I, too, get that chance," I respond, pressing his strong fingers under my softer ones. "A slave never gets that chance." The skin at my nape itches where my barcode is burnt into my skin and I fight the urge to touch it. Instead, I run my other hand up Jax's bare arm, enjoying the muscles, strong and defined.

"So maybe the calendula isn't such a miserable thing," he says, a small smirk breaking out on his face. "In the big picture."

I blink rapidly. "You're right. I will just need to be creative and try again." Except this *is* a competition... although I cannot tell him. It's not me against the other humans, though—not exactly. More like it's me versus my fate once they all find out I can't bear young. If I haven't achieved enough wins here at my farm, proving that my ag skills are so superior that everyone needs me as a de facto expert, who knows what will happen?

I confide in Jax, "Calendula is sometimes called *Marigold*." I try out the Earth word on my tongue. I don't speak English (nobody does), but still, many of the old words survive, the ones that name the plants that now power the galaxy. "Another slave told me that thousands of cycles ago, on my home planet, it was used in mating ceremonies." I try to imagine what she'd described; thousands of golden, ruddy blooms adorning a dark-skinned bride, her friends, the decorations... making the whole city glow. This Earth information, passed down from slave to slave all these centuries, feels sacred to me. "I don't know if that's true. But the properties of the plant are well known now, anyway." I squeeze his arm.

"And those are?" He's not looking away. Jax always reads me like a holo. His face is alert, like he really cares about what I'm saying.

"It has antimicrobial and anti-inflammatory properties, and I hypothesize that it will be ten times more powerful for Zandian cuts and scrapes than on human skin, based on your reaction to other herbs I've tried."

I run my index finger over a long, thin scar on his arm. He got this one early on when we were clearing a field. I put some botanical oils on it to help it heal, but I have goals to improve the way wounds recover. "Imagine healing so fast you barely have time to cry over it." I shoot him a teasing smile. Of course he never cries; no Zandian males do. Their stoicism in the face of pain is well known. They don't get injured as easily or as severely as humans; when they do, they tolerate it with a warrior's duty.

"Cry over it?" His eyebrows are nearly in his horns, and he growls at me. "Cry? Oh, Riya, I'll give you something to cry about." He furls his brow and steps closer. "Take off your clothes and bend over my lap, sweet earthling."

I squeal and put my hand to my mouth, hiding a giggle. "Are you going to massage my sore muscles? You are such a thoughtful mate. Thank you, Jax."

He smirks. "Massage? I suppose, in a way of speaking, what I plan might be called that. I could use my hand," and he holds up his massive purple palm, and flexes his fingers, "to apply pressure to your ass muscles. Take that as a massage if you want."

But even though his eyes flash with arousal, I see lines around them, too. Is my mate worried about something?

J*ax*

"Your massage sounds very appealing," Riya smiles up at me. She traces her finger along the side of my face. "But first tell me what else is on your mind. I know I'm not the only one who is upset about something this planet rotation."

"What do you mean?" I'm surprised at her insight. Truth be told, I'm entirely frustrated with a situation at work—something new to me. The fact that Riya can read me this well is a shock, and then, a pleasure. I can trust her.

I tug her into my body, and she leans back into my muscles, letting out a breath of air, as if she feels safe.

I shift and look to the North, to the Afir Hills.

"You're quiet." She touches my quad, stroking softly. "Is

anything on your mind?" She stiffens, and I swear it seems like she holds her breath for a second.

"Nothing I want to worry you about." At this, she relaxes again.

She slaps my skin with her fingertips, barely more than a caress. "Nothing to worry me about? Everything about you is my concern, from here to here." She wiggles her ass against my groin and reaches up to stroke the side of my head.

I chuckle, but it trails into a sigh. I admit, "I'm working on a roadway right now, breaking ground for it and determining where it will run."

"The one you discussed the other night," she remembers. "What's the problem?"

"I'm working short term with a team of three other Zandians... not my cousins. The other two, Arran and Ketral, argue all the time. I could say we live on Zandia, and they'd argue." My voice rises despite my intent to stay calm. "I'm trying to compromise, but they lack logic."

She nods immediately. "You, Zandians, are used to rank and order, taking direction without question. Now, you have the ability to question. Your team mates who are giving you a hard time, maybe they're expanding to fit their new lives. They are learning to live without direct orders from a commander. Working as a team of equals is different from working in a ranked system. Based on their experience, your calm, logical discussions might not work. Perhaps they may react better to someone just stepping up and saying, *These are my ideas, and this is why they will work, and this is how it's going to be, unless you can immediately, right now, prove me wrong.*

"That's a fascinating observation, Riya." It all locks into place. "We *are* used to order. In fact, because I was so used to it, I was unable to see outside of it. It's like I was inside a glass box." I hold my hands up, as if defining a space in the air, width and height. "You just set me free."

Her smile is so brilliant, her eyes so glossy with love and happiness, that I kiss her, hard and fast, my exuberance spilling out. "You should have been a captain. Or an advisor to one." My footsteps are light, and I tap her ass with a smirk. The thing is, I'm not making a joke. This woman, this human, is incredible. Every planet rotation she surprises me with new depths of insight, fresh ways to make my life better.

7

Riya

"Riya, I hear that you impressed everyone this planet rotation." Tarren takes a large spoonful of the rice pilaf I've created with tomato, mushroom, and basil, and shovels it into his mouth. It's the weekly pleasure meal, the only actual food my Zandians consume, and I take great pride in presenting them with the most delicious concoctions I can manage.

Jax nods. "If it wasn't for your special herb mixture that stopped the toxic *vipn* saliva from spreading in the wound, Slanic would have lost his leg."

"*Veck*." Ronan slams his fist onto the table, then shoots me a glance and touches my arm. "Sorry, Riya. I'm proud of you. Just angry that the *vipn* attacks are getting more frequent." He shakes his head, then takes a large mouthful of food. It's sort of funny and sweet that once my mates taste my food, there is literally no topic that can turn their stomachs.

I find it hard to swallow, though, and force down my bite, which seems like cardboard in my mouth. "He may not gain full mobility," I caution them, the same words the midwife and I had expressed to King Zander.

I put down my fork and clench my fists together in my lap. "He lost so much blood. And the edges of the wound... they are so destroyed. The teeth of the *vipn* are like razors. They shred." I shudder. "Like the flesh is made of the thinnest paper. His wound will need to be tended regularly to ensure that the edges match up as he heals."

Jax puts his hand over my clenched ones. "But we are lucky to have you. By we, I mean all of Zandia." He gestures with his fork. "You were the only medic who knew what to do." His face shines, and I can see the pride.

"It's my duty," I say, still feeling the adrenaline. Being summoned with an emergency palatial pod at the dome. Standing over Slanic, seeing him writhe in pain, tears of unexpressed anguish in his eyes, the wound as awful as anything I'd seen in battle, the pain worse because of the poisonous saliva of *vipn*.

I had packed my emergency kit of herbs and poultices, including new ones I'd created, things that I believed could detoxify skin. Thank sweet Mother Earth it worked. Even now, I'm shaky with relief, coming down from the high of the situation. King Zander has tasked me with creating more of my balm and asked me to teach all of the other agriculture reps how to create it, so it could be stocked in everyone's dome and in the medbays. I'm proud that my plan to be useful is taking shape.

King Zander and Dr. Daneth had looked at me with such surprise, and then respect, mixed into one, that I almost flew away with pride. Dr. Daneth even asked how it was possible that I could do such things without knowing how to decipher. The truth, which I told him, is that I don't know. As slaves we weren't allowed to read or gain knowledge, but in our tents, the elders taught us everything they remembered, and knowledge was passed down orally. I clung to everything I learned, figuring it was my duty to remember it for the next generation, whether it was seed instructions or healing. And now that I don't need to hide this interest, my brain is constantly creating things, even while I relax.

Tarren takes another great mouthful, nearly as much as I would eat in a meal and inhales it. "You are developing a reputation as being the master botanist," he says. "We will need to hold onto you tightly so no being steals you away." It's a joke, but his eyes are fierce.

I smile and wrap my arms around myself. "I'm not going anywhere," I tell him, meeting his dark gaze. When his slow grin starts, the dirty one that tells me what he wants, I flush. "Unless it's to the hoverdisk," I add, relaxing my solitary embrace, eager for his touch. For all of their touches.

"No." his voice is harsh, and he tempers it with a head duck. "I have somewhere else in mind." He clears his throat, and looks at Jax and Ronan, tilting his head. "Maybe...?"

They nod and Jax smiles. "I think it's overdue."

Ronan jumps up. "Let's go immediately."

"Go where?" I look from one male to the next. "Do you have somewhere special in mind? Are we going to visit Lily? Or maybe search for Agrax bark? You know I believe that it has a special acid in it, a mild one, that can help reduce pain and fevers." I've been asking them to take me to the forest forever, it seems. If I can get another win under my belt with a new medicine, I will feel more secure in my spot on Zandia.

Tarren scowls at me. "Riya, the bark is in a place that's

not safe," he reprimands me, his eyes trained on mine. "We will take you in a week or two when we have time to properly prepare for such a trip and can all three accompany you. Until then, it will have to wait. Is that clear? We cannot risk you going alone, not with vipn attacks on the rise in that area."

I nod, biting my lip. Of course he doesn't understand how important this is to me. And I can't tell him. So I just smile. "Yes," I say, tamping down my anxiety. "So where are we going, then?"

"Where?" Tarren stands up, his massive arms rippling as he stretches. "We're going to take you to see the crystals at the Eloki Waterfalls. It's one of the most beautiful places on the planet. After a planet rotation like today, I think we all need to experience the healing properties. Even if there's no time, we should make time for this."

Warmth curls in my chest. "I have wanted to see this forever!" I jump to my feet, heart racing. "Thank you." I laugh and could even dance from excitement.

The dismal look on Ronan's face floors me, and I stop. "What? What's wrong?"

"Nothing." He swallows. "Except that it took us this long to *vecking* take you to do something fun. Stars, but we're miserable mates. How do you tolerate us?"

"Ronan." I peer at him, trying to decide if he's serious. I put my arms around him. "How can you say that? All of us have been so busy with work. I am well aware that there is barely time for sleep, let alone pleasure trips. I don't consider you lacking," I assure him.

He's still stiff. "We've kept you here alone for lunar cycles without a visitor. We must do better."

"I can hardly complain," I say, tapping his horn, which usually makes him growl and smile at me. "I am sure that in a few solar cycles, things will be so calm that there will be nothing but leisure time, all planet rotation." This thought makes me uneasy, because a few solar cycles from now—where will I even be? I bite my tongue and add, "But today I would love to see the crystals."

I tap his horns again and whisper, in a voice that everyone can hear, "The only concern is whether we'll have privacy at the waterfalls?"

His shoulders relax, and he laughs, then grabs me tightly. "In case we need to *veck* you there, is that what you mean?"

"No, in case we need to discuss land management strategy," I retort, and make a face at him.

He growls and picks me up in his arms. "Be sure to bring some things from the box," he suggests to Jax. "This one is acting very feisty today and may need a reminder of how to talk appropriately to her mates."

I giggle as we head out to our newly delivered pod vehicle, allowing Ronan to carry me. Most of the early domes have shared vehicles now; someday we'll have our own dedicated one, but production times can't keep up with the need, so we alternate.

"Thank *veck* it's our turn for the pod," says Tarren, as he syncs his comm device to the controls and types in coordinates. "And that it's one of the new auto-drive ones."

"Because you're too lazy to captain it," agrees Ronan, nodding.

Tarren snorts. "More because I have to keep an eye on you, to make sure you're not accidentally falling out of the emergency release door or pushing buttons you shouldn't." He rolls his eyes and I laugh. I love their affectionate rivalry. At first, I was worried they really didn't get along. Now I know it's just part of the way they interact, and that their bond goes so deep it can't be shattered, all three of them.

As the pod zooms past our dome, my pulse quickens as new vistas come into view. There are our neighboring domes, and now the Eloki Hill, and—oh, *Mother Earth*.

Tears come to my eyes and I clasp a hand to my mouth, as the most majestic scene confronts me. The waterfall must be hundreds of feet high, and the water is white and snarled, crashing like waves, but from this distance, it also reminds me of lacey flowers in the breeze. Rainbows flash and dance through the spray, and I can already hear the roar, a mountain of water, falling endlessly down into a deep blue pool, cerulean, azure. And on all sides, as far as I can see there are crystals. Caves, grottos, different colors, all sparkling and twinkling like a vast treasure. It's something from a dream.

"It's even better than the holos," I murmur, eyes wide.

"No image does this justice," agrees Jax, taking my hand.

All three of them are silent, and I wonder if this affects them more powerfully than it does me. They have a deep connection with these crystals, which power their blood, their very existence. That was part of what made the Finnian takeover so despicable. They sought to clean this planet out of its crystal completely. Sell it for laser guns. Because they knew Zandians required it to live, they purposely tried to exterminate their entire species.

But their time to pay came.

"It is a sacred place," Tarren says finally. "Can you feel it, too?" His eyes seek mine.

"I do." I touch his face, along the scar. "Yes."

"Your crystals came from here." His voice is low and he touches my ear. I push my head into the warmth of his palm.

Jax cups my nape, running his thumb along the tendrils of hair there. "The crystals are not just for beauty." He drops a kiss onto my neck. "They are a reminder you are as sacred to us as life. You wear the crystals to show that you are necessary to us, for life and our future. It's a bond that can't be broken."

I tear up and put my hand on top of his, so both of our palms press into my body. "Thank you. I have never been so valued in my entire life."

I force my thoughts to stay here, in this moment, not to lurch to the future. "Can we... go out? May I touch the crystals?"

"Let's go." Ronan holds out his hand. "I want you to look at all the colors and tell me which are your favorites, and I will compare and see if mine match. I have a special fondness for the one with hints of red." He smiles at me. "I don't know why, but I just do."

"The moss is thick alongside the waterfall," Jax says. "We can relax there, a safe distance from the edges."

"It's so loud." I almost have to shout to make myself heard. This close to the falls, the power is extraordinary, and terrifying. So much water can crush and destroy anything, even as it's a force for life. Nature is a fierce goddess.

Rocks studded with crystals are interspersed with ferns, scattered amidst the thick moss. I wander to the closest one and run my hands over the crystals, pink and teal, aquamarine and garnet, allowing my fingertips to feel them. Then I close my eyes and touch again, and to my surprise, feel a thrum, a spark, coursing through me.

Startled, I blink and look around—was that real? My mates watch me, hunger in their eyes.

"There's energy here." Jax says with a smile at my reaction. "We all feel it. If you can too, that will only strengthen our bond. I didn't know if a human would feel it, but—we have much to learn about how Zandians and humans interact. Change each other."

They seem even more powerful than before, as if the very air here revitalizes them. I've never seen Ronan stand this tall, or Tarren look this magnificent. Jax's profile is beautiful beyond belief, his muscles perfect.

Jax nods to his cousins. Once again, they communicate without words, and when Jax turns to me and holds out his hand, gesturing to a thick patch of soft moss a few dozen feet away, I smile.

I wasn't sure it would be appropriate. Now that I'm here, mating by this waterfall is not just acceptable, but necessary. This place calls to me. I want to be one with my Zandians, and I can barely contain my arousal as Jax strips me of my clothes, without words. It's too loud to speak, and at this moment, we need no language.

We fall into a rhythm that has become natural, an order we understand from many nights together. And when I come against Ronan's mouth, and with Jax's cock, and then Tarren's, I cry out my orgasms, screaming my joy into the roaring water that swallows my sounds but tosses them back in its echoes across the valley. And what I'm shouting out is this: *I'm happy.*

8

Tarren

"I have exciting news," I call, my heart pounding as I enter our dome, late in the evening. The sky is dark, with the stars and constellations bright like diamonds on black ink. The dome smells like bread, something Riya must have baked this planet rotation. Although I don't eat like she does, I've come to enjoy the welcoming aromas associated with her human habits.

Jax, seated on a stool, his legs spread wide, frowns down at a large map on the table, tapping his fingers in concentration. Ronan lies on a couch, Riya nestled up to him; he's playing her some holo on his Comm tabb. Her eyes sparkle as her hair brushes his shoulder. My cock quivers, imagining her hair on my skin, but—later.

"Katya is pregnant with young," I call out, slamming the door and stamping my boots on the patch of cloth Riya admonishes us to use. "She announced just now."

Jax leaps up and the map drops to the floor in his haste. "What great news," he roars, punching the air with his fist.

Ronan comes over and gives me a rough hug. Then he steps back and laughs. "Well, maybe I should save the embrace for the Zandian who put the baby there," he remarks, and we all laugh, a little too loudly, perhaps. "We should all celebrate. Riya, what do you think?"

But Riya's gone pale, eyes wide, as if in shock. Then she blinks and rubs her hands together. "I'm... beyond myself with excitement," she says, her voice low.

Like *veck*.

Is our little mate sorry she's not pregnant first? Stars, I never want her to feel like a failure. Not at anything.

She touches her face and looks out the window for a moment, and I pick up a wave of unease from her. Is she scared? I look to Jax and Ronan for clarification, but neither have caught her expression, and by the time she rises to her feet and shifts her long hair behind her ears, she's smiling, too, her cheeks back to their regular color.

"It's amazing," she says. "A baby. The future. Of course, we knew it was going to happen."

"But nobody was completely sure," Ronan added. "So it's a relief. The first young in the repopulation project." He grabs Riya around the waist and swings her in a circle. "How about we spend some time tonight making sure we are the second group to announce?" He puts her down and steps back. "Unless... you already... are... expecting?" His eyes go wide, and his face goes still.

I snort, because he's touching her belly like she's made of something fragile.

But she shakes her head. "No. I'm not." Her voice, almost mournful, makes me wonder what's going on in her head.

"Not y*et*," Jax corrects, leaning in to kiss her neck. "But soon."

Ronan is giddy. "Zandian planet, population X plus one!" he shouts, and Riya smiles at him, her eyes regaining their sparkle.

I take a deep breath. It's all coming together, just as we dreamed it all those years ago. Our own planet... homesteads... and now, the promise of a growing population. All the pieces falling into place like some plan by the fates.

The urge to take my mate overwhelms me and I tug Riya into my embrace. "Soon we will see your belly swelling with a child," I growl into her ear. "Mine." I don't know if it will be mine or one of my cousins, and at this moment, I care little, as long as it happens.

"Nothing would make me happier." Her voice sounds faint. She reaches up and traces the scar on my cheek. When she first did this lunar cycles ago, I flinched away, but now I lean into her soft touch, knowing she does it from affection. She enjoys every part of my body, she tells me, and her fingers don't lie. "You are so strong. Noble. Someday you will father a dozen children." Her eyes fill with tears.

"It makes me emotional, too," I admit, reaching back to cup her tight ass. I've learned that not all tears mean anguish—sometimes humans cry when they feel strong emotions, like happiness. I'm proud that I figured it out this time. "But my cousin is right. We should spend some time ensuring it." I grin and smack her where I grabbed her flesh, and she squeaks, that little surprised sound I *vecking* love.

"I heard that humans become more fertile, the wetter they are when they *veck*," Jax announces, stripping his garments. "Riya, that means I'm going to have to spank you nice and hard right now, because we all know that gets you so indecently soaked."

"No..." she moans, but her eyelashes flutter on her cheeks, and I see the telltale flush of arousal on her cheeks. Our little human likes our punishments.

"I think she might need a dose of the strap," Ronan suggests. "She *vecks* so much better when we strap her."

"The strap hurts," Riya complains, but I see her nipples pebble under her thin garment and know she likes it far more than she admits.

I growl and rip the fabric in two and bury her cry of surprise with my mouth. She returns my kiss, tentative, then eager, her hands reaching up to play my horns.

I slap her ass hard. "Not yet," I order her, taking her hands down. "I'll tell you when. Keep them down." I lick her nipples and nip them until she whimpers, her breath coming faster, but she obediently keeps her hands at her sides, even though she squirms under my ministrations.

"She's so obedient," Jax says, his voice hoarse with need. "I love how well we've trained her."

"That's right." I slap her ass again, making her moan. She presses her pelvis to mine but doesn't move her hands out of place. "She's our little sex slave, aren't you, Riya?"

When we first got her, a comment like this would have been insane, especially with her background. Now, though, these words make her arousal grow, because I can smell it in the air.

"Yes, please, I'm yours," she whispers. "Can I touch you?"

"No." I sit down on the hoverdisk and tug her over my lap. "Not until I give permission. And I think tonight all three of us are going to orgasm at least once before you get even one. If you come before you're allowed, I'll use the whip on you."

She stiffens—the whip is the most serious of the implements we have, and she knows it's only for serious infractions. In fact, I've never used it on her in play. But I want to make sure she understands what she needs to do.

"Yes, Master," she whispers.

"Spread your thighs," I order. "Show us your arousal. I'm going to spank you until you're twice as wet, then I'm going to *veck* you hard. You don't get to come, though, until you suck off Jax and let Ronan come in your ass. Do you understand?"

"Yes." She shifts her thighs, and I see new moisture gather in her soft folds. She likes to be teased, even if she hates it at the same time, and her orgasms after a session of denial are so ferocious that she nearly passes out from pleasure. I plan to take her there tonight.

I start out hard with firm spanks, not really warming her up. When I do this, it hurts more, but also arouses her fiercely, and she'll take it as long as I hold down her bucking hips and wiggling thighs. I spank until her ass is pink and she's begging me to stop, then I shift and hold her so she's sitting on my lap, her back against my chest.

"Ow, ow, Tarren, ouch," she says, pushing her head into my shoulder. "It hurts, are you done? Please *veck* me now!"

"See if she's wet enough," I order Jax, who's already there.

"Can you lean back, lift up her legs, and spread them?" Jax asks.

"I can, cousin." I smile and lean back against the head of the hoverdisk, and tilt Riya's body by grabbing under her thighs and lifting up. "Legs up, human," I order, "nice and high, and spread wide. Do what Jax wants."

She whimpers but obeys, assisting me, displaying herself as ordered.

"Reach down and spread your pussy lips for Jax," I order.

"And if you're not wet enough, you're getting the strap to help."

"I'm so wet," she moans, and reaches down. *Veck*, but I want to be the one tasting her honey right now. My turn will come, though, so I force her legs higher up to give Jax the treat he desires.

He bends down and buries his head between her thighs, licking at her flesh until she cries out and I feel her tremble in my arms. "Jax, Tarren, I'm going to come, please," she begs.

"You know the rule," I growl into her ear. "Are you asking for the whip?"

"No, I don't want the whip, but I don't think I can hold it," she pleads, her thighs pushing against my grip.

"Too bad," I say, without sympathy. "It's part of your training. You have three masters to please, Riya. You need to learn to handle as much as we choose to give you. Orgasms are a reward, today. You earn them by giving us pleasure."

"I want her lying on the edge of the hoverdisk," Jax announces. "Riya, let your head drop down a little at the edge of the hoverdisk, and open your mouth as wide as you can. I'm going to *veck* your throat. If you please me, I'll ask Ronan to lick your cunt as a reward. If you don't satisfy me, he'll spank your pussy instead."

Riya gasps, and I move her to the desired spot. She looks a little scared, but when she spreads her legs she's so wet now that it's dripping down her inner thighs, and her nipples are bullets.

She opens her mouth and shuts her eyes.

J *ax*

I'm so hard it hurts, and the sight of Riya naked and spread, mouth open to please me, is beyond compare. The height is perfect, and I grasp her head in both palms. "Open your eyes," I tell her, and she does, looking at me upside down. "You won't be able to talk with my cock in your mouth," I tell her, "and I'm going to *veck* you for a long time. Squeeze Tarren's hand if you need air, and he'll alert me."

"Yes, Master," she whispers, giving her hand to Tarren, who lies beside her, already tonguing her nipples.

"And keep those thighs wide," I remind her, "so Ronan can punish your pussy if it's necessary. Now open." I slap her cheek, not hard, a possessive tap that makes her gasp, but she opens her mouth.

I sink in, inch by inch, the hot velvet of her tongue like paradise. Her throat is narrow, and the grip of it on my cock, so tight, makes me dizzy with pleasure. I grab her head and hold it, moving her as I *veck*, in and out, getting into a rhythm. I feel her stiffen, and pull out, and she coughs and gasps for breath. Then she looks up at me, and obediently leans her head back and opens her mouth.

I pump her again, this time going deeper, and it's mere seconds before I feel the tingling in my balls. "I'm going to come in your mouth," I roar. "Swallow all of it, Riya. Don't miss a *vecking* drop."

She can't speak but I can see from Ronan's expression that she's wetter than ever, because he starts to lick her clit. Her hips shoot up and he grasps them just as I come hard into her throat, pulsing again and again, one of the best orgasms of my life. Having Riya held down and pleasured while I *veck* her mouth is the most arousing thing I've ever seen, and I roar her name over and over, the feeling overwhelming me.

When I pull out, leaving a trail of rainbow semen on her lips, she gasps for air and tries to push her body into Ronan's mouth. "Oh, please, *veck*, please," she wails, twisting in his hands.

"No," he says. "And if you ask again, I'll have to punish your pussy."

"Do it anyway," Tarren says. "I want to hear how wet it is when you smack it."

"Great idea, cousin," Ronan agrees.

I stagger to the hoverdisk and lay down next to Riya, exhausted, my body still pulsing with pleasure. Tarren's still on the other side, playing with one of her nipples.

"Riya, that was amazing," I mumble, reaching out to squeeze her other nipple.

R onan

"Knees up," I order Riya, and she obeys, placing the soles of her feet on the hoverdisk and adjusting her legs. She knows how I like it by now and gets into the positions I prefer when I order her to do it. My cock swells at the sight of her swollen pussy, but it's her dark little asshole that I plan to take tonight. Her ass, always tight, makes me come so hard, and I love the way she struggles against the pain, before it turns to pleasure for her.

"This is for Tarren," I say, and slap her right across the pussy with the flat of my palm.

She yelps, and her knees slam shut, but the look in her eyes lets me know how much she likes this.

"Legs open," I remind her. "Or maybe we'll make you wait until tomorrow for an orgasm."

"You wouldn't," she gasps, her pupils dilating further.

I raise my eyebrows. "I've heard from other Zandians that orgasm denial is a wonderful way to ensure obedience in their humans," I say. "I think someday we need to see if that's true for you."

"But not tonight," she says, her whole body taut.

"Not if you are good," I agree, and slap her pussy again, harder.

She sucks in a breath and her thighs clench, but her legs remain open.

"Juicy enough for you yet, Tarren?" I ask, slapping her a third time, making this one even sharper.

She moans and jerks her hips up to me. "Do it again."

I dip a finger into her body. "You're so wet, Riya." I slap her a few times, lighter ones, making sure that the last few land on her clit. Her body twists and she cries out, the sound one of pleasure.

"Almost wet enough," growls Tarren, so I slap her again, the sound reverberating around the chamber.

"Over," I say, tapping her hip, "and up on your hands and knees. You know that's my favorite way to *veck* your ass."

"It's my favorite, too," she murmurs, and I groan with the sudden need that surges through my body.

I reach for the bottle of lubricant that is waiting on the cover and press the tip of it to her hole. I squeeze, allowing a good amount of it to squirt into her body. She shifts and mumbles something unintelligible, so I slap her ass and squirt again. By the time I drizzle the lube onto my rock-hard cock, I can barely wait.

"Keep your ass cheeks soft and open for me," I remind her, pressing the tip to her entrance. She clenches up, then relaxes, and I press in.

"Oh," she cries, arousal in her voice, as she always does when one of our cocks enters her ass. I hold her hips steady as I push in, inch by inch, enjoying her wiggles. Once I'm fully seated, just as always, she relaxes into me as her muscles accept my member, making a low moan of appreciation.

"*Veck*, it feels so good to be deep inside you like this," I say, holding her hard enough to leave bruises. "I'm going to *veck* you hard. Remember, you don't get to come, and if you do, you get punished."

"I remember," she gasps. "But I might have to come anyway." She loves being made to wait, though, so I don't feel guilty. She's told us more than once that being forced to hold out results in the best orgasms.

Teasing her is so *vecking* fun—taking her to the edge of her self-control and forcing her to stay there, take it, take whatever I want to give. It's a headrush like no other, and I *veck* her for a long time, drawing my cock out and thrusting in, sometimes reaching down to finger her clit until she grows frantic under my body and I can sense that she's no more than a second from giving in.

We're both sweating by the time I roar her name and thrust deep, coming so hard I see stars, filling her ass with my cum. She's chanting my name, and I don't know if she's begging me for release, or if it's an invocation to the universe to help her hold out. Either way, my orgasm is the most glorious thing in my world and I fall beside her, sated, and hold her in my arms until I can think again.

T *arren*

R iya is so needy now that her eyes are glassy with desire, and her whole body is taut with the need to come. Ronan wipes her ass gently, cleaning her after his *veck*, but I can see that she has only one thing on her mind right now... My cock, that if she's lucky, will grant her an orgasm of her own.

She stares at me, her eyes wide, and I need her just as badly. She's under my skin, she's in my mind, she's the one I think of when I fall asleep and when I awake in the morning. Watching my cousins *veck* her and leave her wanting has made me so hard I can barely stand. She's dying for a cock, and it's mine that will satisfy her. Mine that will please her tonight.

I bend down to lick her, the taste that drives me mad, and then kiss her, and she attacks my mouth eagerly, thrusting her tongue to meet mine, pushing her hips to me.

"Taste yourself?" I ask, and bend down to lick her again, over and over, before pressing my lips to hers. "Taste that pussy, the one we all love so *vecking* much."

"Mmm," she murmurs, sucking my tongue, reaching her hand down to squeeze my cock.

"Yeah, grab it hard, rub it like that," I urge her, as she starts stroking me. "Stick your fingers in your pussy and get your juices all over your hand so it's slick while you stroke me."

She does, and the feel of her wet palm is pure bliss. I can only take a few minutes before I flip her onto her back. "I'm going to go so deep you'll scream," I warn her, kneeling on the hoverdisk and tugging her hips so her ass is on my thighs. I spread her legs and adjust my stance so my cock pushes at her cunt. "Like this, little human."

I press into her body and she cries out, trembling, as I stretch and fill her. Even wet as she is, my cock is so large that I have to move slowly to avoid hurting her as I enter.

"Tarren, so good," she mumbles, tossing her head.

"Squeeze your nipples, hard," I order. "Pull them out from your body until I say to stop."

She does it, taking hold of her hard nubs and tugging.

Her nipples are so pretty, taut and extended—I could watch her do this all planet rotation. "Tarren, please, I need you," she says.

I can tell the tingle in her nipples is at that perfect level to drive her arousal higher. I've learned her body well these past lunar cycles, and I don't want to cause her pain... just a little sting, enough to maximize her pleasure. "Stop there and hold that position," I tell her, "while I *veck* you. If you let go or reduce the pressure, I will not let you come. I want you to feel your nipples aching while your pussy explodes."

"Oh, Mother Earth," she mutters, but keeps the tension on her nipples.

Before, I wanted to strap her, but right now, all I can think about is exploding inside her body. Using her hips as leverage, I *veck* her, slowly at first, then harder, until I know my release is approaching.

"Do you want to come?" I murmur, my voice low and rough.

"Yes!" She's hoarse with need, playing with her nipples for both of us.

"Do you think you were a good little human for us tonight? Did you get wet enough and accept your mouth and ass *vecking*? Did you love every second of it?" As I speak, I thrust harder.

"Yes," she wails. "I'm your good sex slave. I love it when you *veck* my mouth and my ass, I love it all, but please let me come, don't make me wait!"

"If I tell you to wait until tomorrow, or you'll get a whipping, will you wait?"

I tease her clit with my index finger.

She jerks in my hands. "I'll wait if you tell me to, but please, for the love of the planet, please let me come!"

I flick her clit a few more times. "Will you be good for us again tomorrow, and offer up your ass and pussy for spanking and *vecking*? Without arguments?"

"Yes, anything," she says, desperation in her tone.

"Then you may come," I decree. "When I tell you."

I pump her one more time. "Now."

And she screams again and again, body contorting, as I come into her as hard as I ever have. "Tarren," she wails. "*TarrenRonanJax!*" And she crumples up her face and her whole body stiffens, then she goes slack, panting, a sheen of sweat covering her body.

I roar out my orgasm, fire flashing in my eyes, and then collapse beside her, grabbing her to me, as if by holding her tightly, I could keep her with me forever.

When I come back to myself and look around, I note while Riya's lying on my chest, her other hand is in Ronan's. Stretched across the foot of the hoverdisk, relaxed and casual, Jax has one hand on her calf, stroking it up and down. He loves massaging her feet and legs—I smile at our usual positions. Somehow, nobody argues that I'm usually the one to hold her against my body, the one who *vecks* her last.

R *iya*

We lie on the hoverdisk, relaxing. Surrounded by the fiercest warriors on this planet, I revel in the utter safety and comfort they provide. When we are together, I lose all of my fears, all of my ugly past, and just exist in the moment. Joy I'd never known existed.

But now, as we relax together, the world slips back into my brain, settling like a thick fog, sending tendrils of the usual anxiety. I sigh.

Jax squeezes my calf. "Riya..." His voice sounds sated, but also questioning.

"I'm great," I tell him—and it was. "Just relaxing. Making sure my legs still work."

Ronan chuckles. "If they don't, I will carry you around like a large baby."

All three of them laugh, but my unease intensifies when Tarren places a hand on my belly. "Soon, then, you'll be carrying two of them, Ronan—her, and the one she'll grow for us."

I bite my lip, trying not to tense under his palm, feeling less protected now, and more—trapped. Tied up in my own untruths and secrets.

"I never knew life could be like this," Ronan says, his voice musing and soft, pressing my palm to his lips.

"Nor did I." Pain rips through my chest. Mother Earth, it hurts. If I'd been honest with them from the start, I wouldn't be here now, enjoying this intimacy. But in telling the truth, I would have avoided the inevitable conflict that lies ahead of me like a predetermined cancer.

"I think what I like most," Tarren says, his voice slow, like he's feeling out the words as he goes, "is the trust we have built."

Ronan and Jax makes noises of assent as Tarren continues. "The three of us, our bond has only deepened by sharing you, Riya. Having you at our side, working with us, gives me happiness." He pulls me to him for an unexpected kiss on my temple, and I tear up.

Jax caresses my ankle. "Knowing that we don't have to worry about lies, or deceit, that we come home to a place full of safety and affection, it's everything."

Ronan entwines our fingers. "They're right. There are so many beings in the galaxy that are full of misery—even the ones we should be able to trust the most. Like Gunt, stealing crystals from King Zander."

Tarren's grip tightens. "Do not mention that *vecking* piece of excrement to Riya. You dishonor her purity by bringing him up."

I blink rapidly, a cold feeling gripping my chest. "I want to learn about your past. Tell me?"

"He was a dishonest thief who does not deserve to share the same air we breathe. His deception and betrayal cost us dearly and hurt Zandians we care for greatly." Tarren's voice is hard. "He was running the crystal out on every excursion we took with him. We had no idea he was lying to us. Zandians never lie."

Jax massages my toes, something that usually makes me

moan with pleasure and melt into the covers, but this planet rotation I'm stiff. "That's horrible."

"Prison is too good for him." Tarren's body tightens, before he relaxes. "He will never be forgiven, as long as he and I live."

I nod. "I guess some things... are too big for forgiveness." I'm amazed my voice doesn't tremble.

Zandians never lie. How will my warriors ever forgive my deceit?

"Can you pull up a cover? I'm feeling cold."

Ronan jumps down and retrieves my favorite fleece blanket from the side couch he favors. His jaw is red as he spreads it over me. "I like sleeping with it," he admits. "It smells like you. I don't mind at all that you sleep with Tarren most nights, but I sleep better with your scent near me."

I reach out and run my fingers through his hair. "You can sleep with it always. I just want it right now." Even with the cover over me, the cold won't leave my bones.

9

Riya

My breath comes faster as I step outside the dome and look past my gardens, and I squeeze the hand-knife in my pocket to make sure it's still there. Hoisting my canvas sack to my shoulder, I take a deep breath. The scent is of wet earth, moist from a recent rain, and the green smell of my sprouts. My mates are all gone for their daily assignments, and I have plans of my own.

I look back at the dome, seeing the marigolds reflect like fire through the rippling glass, undulating in my field of vision like carpets of orange. I learned the secret to make them grow.

Once I requested the ancient texts to be sent to our comms unit, I began the arduous work of translations. English is a dead language, not just dead but forgotten, but some beings in the galaxy have collected libraries of old things. Scripts from Alexandrine, a galaxy that exploded eons ago, after a small group escaped by pods. Scrolls from the Tarrhexian planet, obliterated in a battle that's long since been forgotten by history. And tomes from Earth, books that long ago expired into dust, but were scanned into electronic form to live on as long as some being deems them worthy of space on some galactic server.

I'm no genius. But I knew I could teach myself to cipher, and I did it. King Zander mentioned that all humans would receive training in time, once a program was created later, but allowed me to try on my own.

I spent hours toiling over the strange symbols, using a word list to translate the archaic phrases into my tongue. Slowly the words came alive, burst into three-dimensional color, as I unlocked—line by line—the advice from human farmers, planters, like me who lived so many years ago.

I have so many things I can teach my friends, but first I need to make sure my gardens are reliable, that what worked once will work time and again. And right now, I need some plants that grow only here, because the mixture of old Earth seeds with Zandian plants is proving to help strengthen the Earth salves and lotions a dozen-fold.

Tarren has forbidden me to go past our property boundaries without him or another mate and has told me I may definitely not—ever—travel alone, until this *vipn* outbreak is understood and contained. Why the population is moving toward the edge of the forest is a mystery, one that is not as interesting to the Zandians as the rehabilitation projects.

I need to get bark from the Argrax bush. I heard rumor that it contains a powerful medicine—salicylic acid—that helps reduce fever and inflammation. If it's true, I am posi-tive that if I can extract acid from the bark, I can include it in a salve that will increase Zandian healing rate by five times.

It's just that the bark is located in the forest where I'm not supposed to go. Still, I have my knife for protection, and, tucked into my sack, an acidic mixture I created, which I keep tightly capped in a glass vial. Chemical warfare for one. I would be loathe to hurt a living being, but just in case...

In the back of my mind an idea grows, imagining this fluid sprayed large-scale onto an enemy ship, weakening the metal, causing the thing to split open like ripe seed pod in fall, brown and brittle. Maybe I will become Jax's warrior general, after all, someday.

I shake my head and regrip the knife. It's silent but for the trills of the Barillia, brightly plumed birds whose raucous call awakens us in the morning, birds that are not for eating, as their flesh is bitter and caustic. Their eggs, however, are divine—and I've discovered the shells, crushed into a fine powder, make a good fertilizer for herbs.

A sound makes me dart my head around, but it's just a branch blowing in the wind. My pace is fast, my legs strong on the uneven ground. The woods are only seven miles away from the dome, but it's another world, a place I never get to see. Even though I'm nervous about disobeying, and on constant lookout for *vipn*, the exultation of a solo adventure fills me with giddy joy, and I whoop and race ahead, feeling my hair stream out behind me, as free as I've ever been.

Medic work made me strong, and my daily tasks keep my muscles toned and tight, and I find that running a distance isn't taxing. Yet as I approach the dark, misted reaches of the forest, I slow down, panting, and look around for danger. Seeing nothing extraordinary, I approach, keeping my footfalls soft and easy, eyes looking for my prize.

The Agrax is an epiphyte; it grows wound around other trees, roots exposed, absorbing what it needs from the misty air, using the host as a prop to stay off the forest floor. They favor the forest entrance, where the sunlight is stronger, but not the direct edge, because it's too dry. I'm not too worried about the beasts, because they prefer the other part of the woods, where it's darker and more protected. Still, they've been venturing out further these days, so I need to be on the lookout.

Another slave told me on Earth, all those thousands of years ago, my ancestors tracked animals on foot, using prints, tracks, scat, and crushed grass to tell the path as clearly as if the animal stood up and called out the location. If only I could do that for the plants I need.

I hold the knife at the ready, my fist tight, ready to strike if necessary, but nothing comes, and as I advance slowly into the gloom, my heartrate calms, and I'm able to look around me and examine the area as a botanist.

Moss on the sides of the trees—all the same side. Needles from trees, leaves underfoot, making a cushioned mat. Bright blue fungal growths snarled in protruding roots —could that be Lissa, a mushroom that's toxic when raw, but when cooked, releases a potent medicine that can aid sleep? I crouch down and cut some with my knife, allowing it to fall into a clean container that I seal up, then cleanse the knife on moss. I know better than to touch it with my bare fingers.

As I venture further, the air grows moist and a floral smell lingers. There are no bird calls here, just the crunch of debris under my feet. I pause as a shadow passes over the sun. It's a long way back, and I need to leave soon if I want to stop by Holla's dome on the way back home. She has herbs I need, not for a project, but for myself. If I stay on schedule, I can fit it all in and still beat my mates back home to avoid questions.

It's then that I see it—the epiphyte I need. "I found you!"

I exclaim. I pull another vial and scrape the loose, papery bark into the container. To my surprise, it rolls up into little scrolls, and it's easy to get a lot of it.

I put on gloves and carefully unwind a smaller Agrax from the branch it has claimed, careful not to tear roots or rip leaves. It's not toxic, but I don't want to damage the fragile plant. I wrap it in a piece of lintless cloth and place it into my bag. If this bark is useful, I may be able to figure out how to make this bush grow back in my dome. I extricate another.

It's then, as I turn to place the second Agrax in my bag, success flooding my brain with liquid gold, that I see the eyes of *vipn*. Red eyes, three pairs, one much lower to the ground. A young? What are they doing here?

I crouch and freeze, knife tight in one hand, the Agrax in the other, like a sword. My heart speeds up until it's a blur of energy. I'm on a hair trigger, ready to react. The animals look as intent as I feel, and then the young one gives a raspy mewl of pain that is unmistakable. At that, the two taller animals bend down, one of them yelping in reply; the second looks back up at me and growls, a long, low angry snarl, and I see long teeth, wet with saliva. Poisoned saliva?

I cannot risk getting bitten. I drop the Agrax and reach into my satchel, feeling around until I grasp the smooth glass of my acid vial. Holding it at the ready, I wait, sick to think I could destroy an animal, even a vicious one, yet I know it may be necessary to save my own life.

The young one whimpers again and licks its leg—I can see clearly now that my eyes have adjusted. I notice something else—their scratch marks, claw marks, on the trunk of a tree where an Agrax grows.

I stand my ground, and inspiration strikes— without looking away from the animals, as if breaking eye contact will allow them forward, I shift the vial in my hand, crouch down, touch the Agrax with my fingers where I dropped it, and peel off a long strip of the thin bark. It curls up in my hand, releasing a pleasant, woody aroma. I toss it towards the trio.

The taller one growls more loudly, and howls, and my thighs quiver. But then it darts forward and grabs the bark in its mouth and retreats, dropping the bark at the foot of the other adult. She (I assume it's a she) chews the bark, soft slick slurpy crunches, and then, to my surprise, bends down to spit the mouthful on to her young—onto its leg.

Sweet Mother Earth! These intelligent beasts are using medicine to heal!

I step forward, hoping to leave while they're occupied, but the larger one snarls and acts like it is going to leap, and I freeze. I repeat my action; prying off a piece of bark, tossing it forward.

This time the larger one chews the bark, and when I move past their group, they don't stop me. A few more feet, and I race as fast as I can, still holding my knife and the branch and my vial, not pausing to look back, until I am a mile out, then two, and I can barely breathe, heading toward Holla's homestead.

I whirl around, half-expecting to see a hoard of furry monsters racing at me, fangs bared, but the field is empty, so I run again until my chest burns. I bend over, panting; when I look up, a sparkling dome refracts the sun into my eyes in a thousand shards, and I realize that I made it to Holla's place. I lope up, and when she sees me, her whole face drops in shock and dismay.

"Riya!" She extends her arms for a hug, sees my knife, draws back. "Come into the dome." She tugs my arm. "What are you doing out here, alone? Are you hurt?" She sits me down on a wooden stool. "What in Mother Earth is going on? Where are your mates?"

She glances out the dome at the tall grasses blowing in the wind, then to me. Even in my exhaustion, I'm careful to put my Agrax, my vial, and knife, back into my pack.

"I was running," I rasp, and grab at my water packet.

"Save yours, I'll get more," she offers, and she fetches me a pitcher. Water never tasted so good. I suck it down, greedy for more, and she refills it.

Finally sated, I look at her. "Thank you," I say. "I need your advice."

She nods and takes a breath. "I expected you to come. But not like this." She gestures at my sweaty, wild appearance. "What's in your satchel?"

"My salvation," I murmur, and I'm grateful she doesn't ask me what I mean.

"So?" She quirks one brow.

"I would like to..." The words won't come. "I need..."

She waits, silent, still.

"I cannot bear young." I force out the sentence. "Is there any way you can help?"

Her eyes, so full of sympathy, meet mine. "That depends," she says, "on the reason for the infertility."

"Shock sticks." I stick up my chin. "My fallopian tubes were scarred." I squeeze my eyes for a second. "From all the electricity, over time."

"Oh, Riya." Her face falls. "I'm so very sorry." The look in her eye tells me what she's about to say next.

"There are herbs," I begin, grabbing her hands, leaning forward. "Old traditions." My voice shakes, and I realize I'm squeezing her fingers too hard, panting into her face. I release my sweaty grip. "Things the slave elders spoke of. I don't grow them, but I think you do."

"Those work for specific ailments." Her voice is gentle. "There are herbs to bring on menses that have failed, and salves that can make a woman more fertile. However, if she is not fertile at all to start, the herbs will have no efficacy."

"I need to try them." I tap my foot.

"Riya." She looks down. "The damage done by shock sticks is... irreversible." She speaks slowly, as if to a child, but her voice is kind. "No herb can undo that. I'm sorry."

"But it might not be that!" I stand up and pace, throw my arms out as if to explain. "It could be something else, and they just thought it was that." I wrap my arms around myself. "The Ocretions are notorious liars, and sloppy, too, when they don't care about a slave any longer. It's possible that it's... reversible. Even if it's a tiny chance, I need to try." Tears sting my eyes, and the exhaustion of the journey falls onto me like a stone. I sink back to the stool and bury my head in my hands before looking at her. "Please."

She puts up a hand. "But first I need to understand your body, Riya. When do you feel the stabbing pain of ovulation, or do you never feel it? I need to understand the timing of your menses. And I'll need to ask about..."

"Please. Without the questions. I need the herbs." These are things I have not grown, although I know of them. They are not seeds that were included in my pack, and if I ask for them, others might ask why I need them. I've become somewhat of an experimenter, but I don't want to risk questions.

I come closer and take her hands. "Please."

She blinks and cocks her head, and then comes closer, until we're almost nose to nose, looking into each other's eyes. It's not intimate in the same way I am with my mates, but it's closer than I've been to another human.

"Have you been eating apples?" She steps back, looking

at me, and darts a glance at my belly, then back up to my face.

"Apples? Mother Earth, I wish." I smile. "Won't it take years to grow a single tree? How I'd love one, though." We grew apples on the agrifarm, but I was never allowed to eat them. Still, we sometimes ate the rotten ones discarded by the slave masters.

"Hmm." She bites her lip. "I wonder."

"What?" I put a hand to my lower back. I'm not accustomed to running and my body aches. I stretch out my calves. "I need to get back home soon."

"I will give you the herbs," she says, finally, and retrieves a packet of dried leaves from her supply. "They cannot work for the ailment you describe. They can, however, strengthen a pregnancy, and I am only giving it to you so you feel like you are doing everything you can."

"Thank you."

She says, "You have not told your mates."

We look at each other for a second. "Can I trust you?" My voice cracks.

She takes my hand and folds the packet into my fist. "Know that I will always act in what I believe is the best interest," she says, and this is as close as I will come to a promise of secrecy. I don't wish to delve into what *best interest* means, and whether it's mine, as long as I can have what I came for.

"Thank you." I squeeze her hand. "I will repay you."

She shakes her head. "You do what it takes to make your homestead and your family successful, and that is repayment for everything."

I nod. "I need to go." I stow the packet into my satchel alongside my other treasures.

"Riya, no." Her voice is firm. "It's getting dark and it won't be safe. My mates will accompany you home."

"No! I'll get myself back." I stand up, my tone fierce, and hurry out, hoping I'll make it back before my mates come in for the night.

J*ax*

"R*iya!*"
Tarren, Ronan, and I call at the tops of our lungs. We returned to the dome to find her gone. Simply gone.

My mind is going *vecking* crazy trying to figure out where she's gone. What could've happened to her.

She knows better than to leave the site. We've warned her many times. I'm cursing the fact that we never gave her a comms cuff so we could communicate with her or track her, but it simply wasn't necessary. Not when she never strayed from our homestead.

What the *veck*?

"Riya! Riya!" Tarren's voice has gone hoarse. He's already at the crest of the hills far from our homestead.

What if she's been bitten by a vipn? Or abducted by some intruders? What if—oh *veck*—what if she fell in the mine?"

"I'll check the mine!" I shout to Ronan and run for the opening.

"Wait! Jax!"

I stop and whirl. Ronan points at a dot on the landscape. A small figure hurrying out of the damn forest.

My heart leaps into my throat. It's Riya—it has to be. But what if it's not? No, it is.

All three of us run for her.

Tarren gets there first and I pity Riya, because Tarren— when he's mad—is a fearsome being to behold. Not that he'd ever harm her. But his sheer size and now the facial scar makes his visage terrifying when he glowers. And he is furious. I can tell by the set of his shoulders, the stomp of his feet. He'd been the most frantic out of the three of us—if you can quantify such things. His need to protect her and the helplessness of not knowing where to find her made him crazy with worry. And yes—there she goes up over his shoulder. Tarren claps his meaty hand down on her upturned ass as he carries her inside.

Ronan and I meet them at the dome, not that Tarren's waiting for any being.

"Where have you been?" I demand, but Tarren carries our upside-down mate into the chamber. "To the forest? To look for Argrax bark?"

"I-I..."

I'm trying to make sense of what happened, but Tarren's still in warrior mode. He drops her onto her feet, quickly spinning her to face away from him. He pins her hands to the wall with one hand and starts to paddle her ass with his palm, fast and hard.

"Ow! Ah," She cries out, but I hear no indignation, and believe me, I'm listening for it. Because we don't even know her story yet and Tarren's already taking his frustration out on her ass.

No, she knows she deserves this, whatever she's done. And I'm fairly certain I was right.

I pull a hoverchair around and sit, watching Tarren's punishment. Ronan joins me in his own seat. The spanking isn't too harsh, but Riya's squeaks and cries are real. I suspect she's more afraid than hurt.

I don't blame her. Even I don't choose to tangle with Tarren when he's mad, and I've known him my whole life.

He spanks over her clothing, not bothering to strip her. I won't make the same mistake. And yes, I do plan on punishing her next. I think we should each choose a punishment, because she scared the horns right off our heads.

As Tarren spanks her, the tension goes out of his face and the cords in his neck stop straining. I'm about to tell him it's enough, but he seems to arrive at the same conclusion. He releases her and walks away without another word.

Riya stays in the position he left her, trembling. Her breath rasps in fast and hard. Her surrender, her submission here, has my cock throbbing. My anger and irritation are completely gone. Now it's just about pleasure. My pleasure. Her punishment.

I stand up and stroll to her side, leaning against the wall where she's still propped, her ass out and ready. Maybe she thinks Tarren's going for an implement. Maybe she's just afraid to move without permission.

"Take off your clothes, Riya." My voice comes out silky soft, laced with danger and the promise of more pain.

She eases her hands from the wall and faces me, entreaty in her expression. Her lower lip trembles.

I stroke my thumb down her cheek. "You know why Tarren's so angry?"

Her eyes dart to my cousin, who's turned to stone where he sits in the corner.

Her head wobbles around like she's not sure whether to shake it or nod.

"Because he was so afraid. We didn't know what happened to you, Riya. We feared for your life." I tilt my head in Tarren's direction. "So this is what happens when you scare a giant warrior. You get a sore ass and a being who will require a very, very long cock suck to forgive you."

I meant it to be sexy, but Riya's eyes fill with tears.

I pull her into my arms. "Shh, sweet girl. He'll get over it. We all will. But first we need to talk. And then there's your punishment to discuss. And I believe I gave you an order." I arch a brow at her.

She scrambles to take off her clothing, our strong little mate so contrite. I have to squeeze my cock through my pants to take the edge off my erection.

I sink back into my hoverseat to watch. "That's it, beautiful," I say when she finishes, and open my thighs. "Come here."

She stands in front of me, awkward and blushing, her fingers knit in front of her pussy.

I pull them apart. "Hold them behind your back. I need to see what belongs to us."

She sucks her lower lip in between her teeth, which nearly makes me groan. I want to be the one nipping that lip. Soon enough.

"So where were you, Riya? You went for Argrax bark?"

She nods and her little tongue darts out to moisten her lips. "And to Holla's."

My gut twists. Our mate has been too lonely here. Lonely enough to sneak off without permission.

I show nothing on my face, though. "You knew we didn't wish you to go in the forest unaccompanied." It's a statement not a question.

"Yes... Master."

Damn. That has me grabbing my cock again and I don't

RENEE ROSE & REBEL WEST

think she even meant it to turn me on. She's simply defaulted to slave mode, which should make me hate the moniker. But I *vecking* love it. Almost as much as I love the submissive tone and having her standing before me naked. Because our mate isn't weak. She's a strong female who just traveled through the forest and located her friend all on her own.

"I know I speak for my cousins when I say we're so *vecking* relieved you made it safely. But that doesn't mean we won't each punish you for putting us through such a fright. You didn't even try to leave us a message?"

She rubs her pretty lips together. "I'm sorry."

I stand from the hoverseat. "Ten with the strap. That's my punishment for you. Spread your legs and bend over at the waist." It's not too cruel. We give her the strap on a regular basis, just for play, but I'll give it a punitive tone. But when she obeys, and I get a glimpse of her pink, glistening core, punishment flies out the window. Oh, I'll make her hurt, but I'm sure all of us will enjoy it. She rests her hands on her knees, but I think she could use a little reassuring contact, so I say, "Ronan, perhaps you'll come over to steady her."

Ronan grins. He, too, has lost all his ire. He sweeps his hoverchair in front of Riya and cups her chin, lifting her face to his. When she starts to straighten her back, he makes a disapproving sound in his throat and she adjusts, arching her ass out to me and lifting her face to him at the same time.

He runs his thumb over her lips. "Good girl, Riya."

I snap the leather across her ass. She jumps and squeaks. Ronan holds her face captive, forcing her to look up at him, to be seen.

I let it swing again and again, laying stripes down her

already glowing ass while Ronan pinches her nipples with one hand, and thrusts the thumb of the other between her lips. I finish her strapping and let the leather fall.

The scent of her arousal fills the room. I don't want to wait another *vecking* moment to put my cock in her.

"What's your punishment?" I rasp to Ronan.

A wicked smile curls his lips. "I'm going to *veck* her hot little ass. She should know that when she's punished, she always takes it in the ass. And we won't let her come, either."

"No, she doesn't deserve to come, does she?" I agree.

I look over at Tarren, who's still looking disgruntled on his seat on the hoverdisk.

I reach my arm around Riya's waist and lift her to stand, her back pressing against my front. With my lips at her ear, I say, "You need to go suck Tarren's cock until he's smiling again. And while you do it, Ronan's going to *veck* your ass. But don't you dare come, little mate, or I'll whip you again with the strap. Understand?"

She nods, her tongue darting out to moisten her lips. All three of us groan.

Tarren wastes no time stripping and lying down on the hoverdisk and Riya dutifully crawls up between his legs. I take my cock out and fist it, watching Riya take Tarren's member into her mouth and Ronan position himself behind her to take her ass.

Veck, I might just come from watching, but I don't want to. I'd rather come in her juicy little pussy. Still, as their sounds grow louder and needier, I have to beat my cock harder and my balls tighten.

For all his surliness, Tarren finishes first, his roar shaking the damn dome. When Riya licks him clean and pops off, I grasp her hair and pull her head up. "Do *not* come," I warn her just before Ronan's shout echoes off the glass and metal.

She whimpers, but obeys, her body going slack, into a purely receptive mode.

"Good girl," I purr. I can hardly wait for Ronan to finish and pull out. I stand at the ready, clothes off, a wet washcloth in hand to wipe her clean.

I flatten her to her belly on the hoverdisk, my palm at her nape. "Spread your legs, beautiful. It's my turn, and I'm tired of waiting for the sweetness that awaits me." I rub the head of my cock in her juices. One thrust and I'm deep, right where I want to be. I groan. "Mmm, this pussy's always so wet for me, isn't it?" I croon, my eyes already rolling back in my head.

Riya's back heaves with her quickened breath. Tarren captures her wrists and pulls them over her head, not that she was trying to use them, just to exert his dominance.

I pull out and slam back in. Riya lets out a keening cry. "Jax," she pants. "Please?"

"*No.*" I make my voice hard. "What did I say?" I pump harder. Faster. "Do you get to come, naughty girl?"

"No," she whimpers.

Oh *veck* she feels so good.

"That's right." Somehow, I'm able to keep up my monologue. "When you're being punished you don't get to come. You'll have to sleep all night with your pussy and nipples throbbing because we're not giving you satisfaction.

She moans. Her muscles tighten around my cock.

"Are you coming?" I snap.

They tighten more. "Uh..."

"*Bad. Girl.*" I slam in so hard she has to brace her arms against Tarren so she doesn't shoot across the mattress.

My words don't matter, though, because we're both

coming. The chamber blurs for me, stars dot my vision. I give an enormous shudder at the end of my release and work to slow my breath.

"Don't ever leave us again, Riya," I croak.

I mean it this time. I'm not playing at punishment.

If she ever left us, I don't know how we'd recover.

A shiver runs through Riya and something pricks my conscious. Something I should pay attention to, but I can't quite figure out what it is.

All I know is that Riya requires something more from us, and not in the sleeping chamber. We're missing some important piece to making her happy.

I need to solve it. Soon.

10

Riya

I step out to my lab, a small workdome where I start my seedlings and work on projects. The males set it up for me not long after we arrived, as a favor, not sure what I'd do with it. But their smiles, once indulgent, soon turned to looks of pride as I became adept at creating things. They enter with respect now, and nod with approval when I tell them of my successes. This is no longer just a hobby, but my mission, and every time I provide something new for the homesteaders, our whole team is proud. Lately I devote more time than ever to my efforts.

When they gently scold me for my late nights in here, trace the tired shadows under my eyes with concerned fingers, I laugh and look away, stating that I want to work as hard as they do and help our planet succeed. And if I don't hide my mania completely, I hope they attribute my frantic need to succeed as my nature. After all, they are competitive at core, and understand ambition.

This planet rotation my mates occupy all my thoughts.

Thank our long-lost Mother Earth they showed me mercy in their punishments last night.

When Tarren first picked me up, I experienced genuine fear. My mates love me, yes, but I hadn't tested them before.

Now I'm absolutely certain of their love.

Which only twists up my gut all the more. Every planet rotation that passes draws me closer to the day I'll have to leave them. Closer to the day they figure out I'm not a suitable mate, because they deserve someone who can give them honesty... and young. In such a short time, they've become my entire universe. I seriously don't know how I'll survive without them.

But, on the bright side, my troublesome trip is yielding information fit for a king. I exclaim to myself as I tap the fine, white powder from my separation cloth, letting it fall in a chalky stream into a clean container.

"Mother Earth." It's a prayer, although I don't pray, and a sign of gratitude to life for granting me this bounty.

I've figured out the Agrax and separated out the precious acid into a soluble salt. When added to a lotion, it will provide pain relief to wounds and aching muscles. When taken internally, it can cure pain. Dr. Daneth has so many amazing things from around the galaxy, but I'm sure that my concoction can stand alongside them. After all, it's from nature, and it's free from side effects. And it will scale nicely into mass production, if we choose, to be readily available to all Zandians.

I pored over Dr. Daneth's holo file of known medicines, and this one is not in the log. It used to be used on Earth long ago, with only mild success listed, so it was never proliferated around the galaxy. But knowing what I do about how Zandian skin is far more sensitive to certain Earth botanicals than humans, I believe it will be ten times more effective than it was for human bodies. Maybe more!

Tired now, even in my exuberance, I stow away my equipment for later use.

"Riya?" Ronan knocks at the door, then enters. "You're always in here. I miss you in the evenings." He gives me a mock sad gaze. "You're much prettier than my two cousins, and you know I would never want to *veck* them."

I burst out laughing. "Yes, thankfully."

"Did you hear the news?" His face lights up as he pulls me into an embrace, his strong arms pulling me close to his strong chest.

I snuggle up to him and kiss his collarbone. "What news? Did you do the impression of Tarren on the job site this planet rotation and make everyone collapse with mirth?"

"No." He taps my ass. "Your smart mouth will get you into trouble, little human."

"Maybe I like your kind of trouble." I push my body into his.

He growls, and then, as if unable to focus until he gets the words, out, he pulls back to look at my face. "Riya, three more human women have announced their pregnancies. That makes six already. And by the way Zorra's mate was smiling, I am nearly positive that she is growing a young, too, but he didn't want to say." His smile is wide, and he is nearly dancing with glee. "I just know we'll be next. I can feel it."

My fingers twitch. Every one of the early teams is now expecting a child... except ours. My stomach churns and I feel bile in my throat and swallow it back down with some difficulty. "That's a blessing," I choke. "How wonderful for Zandia."

Instead of looking up at him, I press my cheek to his bare chest, feeling the thump of his heart, steady and even. Strong. Powerful. His body is so compact and beautiful, so perfect to sire a child who could take up arms for this planet.

"Every human has their own schedule." Ronan's voice sounds sober now and strokes my shoulders. "It doesn't matter who is first, or how long it takes." He still seems confident, happy. I wonder how long it will take before the tone in his voice changes to a question, then to anxiety— weeks? Lunar cycles? "You will be soon."

My stomach knots. "Of course." My breath puffs against his skin. "Every being is unique."

Some of us have been ruined.

"And," he adds, tipping my chin up with his finger to smile into my face, "We should get in some more practice, just to ensure that we are doing everything we can."

"You should practice licking me to orgasm," I suggest.

Please. Distract me from this pain.

"And use your nice, thick Zandian cock to drive me insane with desire." I cup him with one hand, relishing how he gets even harder under my touch. "You know I adore your malehood," I whisper, biting his nipple.

He roars and slaps my ass, then orders, "Do it again. Harder."

I smile and lick his skin, then bite down again, feeling him tense under my touch. Maybe my Zandian likes a rougher touch himself, sometimes? I smile. "Want me to spank you, Ronan? I don't mind. Just bend over, and hand me that strap—"

I scream in delight as he scoops me up and tosses me over his shoulder, landing a flurry of slaps on my thighs. "Spanking is on the agenda, but it will be on your ass, not mine. And just for asking, I'll use the strap on you, sweet human."

"Oh, no, please, I'll be good," I beg, but we both know I love it when he straps me for pleasure.

R *iya*

"Is something on your mind?" Tarren puts his hand across my shoulder and squeezes.

"No." *Yes.* The same thing always circling my mind. I'm driving myself mad with stress. "Just enjoying the sunset. Look at the sky, how the oranges and blues merge together." I survey the distance. "As if they're melting. And then sparkle on the horizon. I learned the dust in the air, crystal dust, is what gives the sky that special shimmer at dusk."

"You are turning into a scholar lately." There is no disapproval in his voice, at least none that I can hear, but I stiffen under his touch.

How can I explain that studying has become an obsession for me now? I have to prove my worth somehow.

"Does that bother you?" I keep my voice light, but focus on the distance, watching as the edges of the purple mountains glisten, their outlines a sparkly darker line.

"Riya?" He touches my chin. "You seem..." he hesitates, possibly searching for a word. "Troubled, lately."

I blink fast and smile. "I'm just motivated to work hard."

"You work hard enough for three beings," he declares, the first sign of frustration breaking through his even tone. "I am concerned that you don't get enough rest. I noticed that lately you rise far earlier than you ever did, sometimes well before the sun is risen. I've heard humans require more sleep than we do, and you're not getting it."

My stomach bunches up in knots. "I hope you're not suggesting that I stop my work in the lab with plants." I cross my arms.

A flicker of surprise gives way to a stubborn scowl. "Of course not! But something is making you restless, and I want to know what it is."

I bite my lip and look away, unable to meet his eyes. There is a subtle tension in our dome now, and I can't tell if it's all caused by me and my worries about being the only first homestead human not to be pregnant or not. But my mates must have it on their mind; everyone talks constantly about who's expecting young, and when, and by whom. It's exhausting to keep smiling when I want to scream and toss myself onto the ground and weep with despair at the whole thing.

How did I possibly think I could do this? A wave of nausea hits me, and I put my hand to my mouth.

"You're pale," Tarren says, touching my cheek. "Are you eating enough?" I see him dart a quick glance down at my flat belly, and then back up to my eyes, as if he didn't want me to see him looking.

"I'm eating fine. All the right nutrients for... that are recommended," I stumble, not wanting to bring it up. I'm eating the right diet to prepare for pregnancy. One that cannot happen, though.

"Are you concerned about... not..." He touches my stomach, spreads out his fingers. The warmth makes me catch my breath, and I feel the usual surge of arousal, but the topic makes me unhappy.

"No," I snap, and try to soften it by touching his face,

tracing his scar. "You will be an amazing father someday, Tarren, and I mean that from the bottom of my heart." *It won't be with me, but it will happen.* To my horror, tears well up in my eyes and I blink. "I'm just preoccupied with a class I'm putting together on stem grafts and propagation for the other dome humans," I lie.

Tarren sighs. "You know you can trust me—all of us."

"I do know that." I lean into his arms.

"Then please trust me with what is troubling you."

"I told you already. Just the classes, and some things I want to accomplish in my lab."

"Is there something we're not providing for you?" He looks into my eyes. "You are unhappy, Riya, I can see it. Are we not giving you what you need?" He pauses. "To be successful as a bonded team for the future, we need to be honest with each other. It's what honorable beings do."

Right. Because Zandians don't lie. How will they feel about all my deceptions, then? Every day I dig myself deeper and deeper.

To my shock, I see uncertainty in his gaze. How is it possible that this strong, fierce Zandian, who has protected and served his planet with honor, defeated a thousand enemy warriors, can feel less than confident?

I don't have it in me to give him any further lies, so I turn away. "Everything is fine," I tell him, my voice low. "I just want to be alone to think about my projects."

He is silent, and then he touches my arm once and walks away, leaving me to the sunset. Now I let the tears fall, and the colors refract like a thousand shards of glass through the droplets, as the sun hovers and then sinks fast over the edge of the world.

11

Jax

"You want what?" But King Zander turns aside and holds up a hand for me to wait. He is down at the loading dock, giving orders. "Did you optimize the genetics for the next teams?" He's speaking to Dr. Daneth via holo-chat. "This round will be more sensitive, because although we wish to have mates set up for ideal genetic matches, we don't want to force humans or Zandians into life-long situations they despise." He runs a hand across his mouth.

I step away because I'm sure I'm not supposed to over-hear this sensitive information.

After some short discussion with the doctor, he closes the holo and turns to me. "Jax."

"My lord." I bow.

"How is your repopulation effort going?" He raises one eyebrow, and not for the first time, I get a strange feeling in the pit of my stomach at the question. At first, it was a fun thing to discuss, the idea of young. Now, I force myself not to snarl.

I shake my head. "No news yet, but I'm sure it will happen soon." I force a smile. "There is no lack of... coupling, in our dome." We're insatiable, all of us. I cannot even count the times.

But something makes me blurt, "King Zander... weren't you going to send us Riya's slave records? So we'd have her history?"

She doesn't wish to talk about her past, and we never force her—I don't wish to trigger her past memories. But I feel that if we learned more about her, we could be better mates to her.

I can't describe the feeling I get from Riya lately. We're all wound up, eager to work hard, anticipation and anxiety filling our chests by turn, but there's something about her that seems melancholy. When she stares out a window, her hand propped on her chin, seeing something a million miles distant inside her mind. I think there is something she needs from us that we are not providing. Is she unhappy with us? Are we not enough for her? When I ask her if anything is wrong, she is quick to say no and distract me with a comment or a kiss. Maybe the documentation holds a clue.

"Oh, did the data never get sent?" Zander turns and voice commands another holo to open. "I'll have them bring it now and pack it with your things. I fear my assistant was busy with settlement planning."

"It's not a rush," I say, and flex my fingers, although if I had it my way, he'd go fetch it immediately.

Zander's mouth quirks into a small smile, as if he can read my mind. "Everything is a rush," he corrects. "But some things need more of a rush than others." He hands me a box. "Here are more heirloom Earth seeds for Riya. These arrived last planet rotation—rare ones I obtained from Midraxx. Lamira's already growing starts in the palace. Riya can consult with her if she needs to, but I imagine she'll know what to do with them."

Pride at my mate swells in my chest, as if I have anything to do with her concoctions. "Before you arrived, Dr. Daneth was raving, as much as he does, about her salicylic acid preparation. He says it's the most novel thing he's seen in years. He offered her this."

He adds a holo reader to the box. I open it and see strange symbols, numbers. "Math?" I tilt my head.

"And chemistry. She understands it, apparently—and has already done things on her own, without training, that experienced chemists struggle to do. Dr. Daneth said she could have been a scholar, a real doctor, if she wasn't born a human. I mean, a slave. Maybe she still can be. She's smart. Take good care of her."

"I do. We do. Always."

R*iya*

"So I'll see you on the EM holo call this week?" Lily's smile brightens her entire face. I'm visiting her in the capital because Jax had to come and pick up some equipment. He figured I'd like to come along and see my human friends.

I shake my head. "I'm not... expecting. So I wasn't planning on it. I have a lot of work to do, anyway."

"Are your mates working you too hard?" Lily's delicate features turn to a frown. "I wouldn't have thought it of them, because they have a reputation for being fair, but if it's too much you can always—"

"It's me. I have set difficult goals for myself." I touch her arm. "My mates have been nothing but kind and support-ive." A flush stains my cheeks as I think about just how supportive in the sleeping chamber.

"Oh, that's a relief." She smiles, but looks at me with tilted head when I don't join in. "Is there something wrong?"

"No. I just don't want to join the holo meeting if I have nothing to add."

"But you will be an Expectant Mother soon, Riya! Even I may be able to conceive. When I was sterilized to become a sex slave, they made the procedure reversible. So Dr. Daneth performed a surgery and now... we're trying."

She blushes.

"I didn't know you wanted to have babies. But I suppose it's required of all of us now?"

Lily frowns. "I don't know if it's *required*. But I guess I do feel like I should do my part. Rok would make a great father, and every baby born will be a step to prevent their species from becoming extinct.

"But the meeting isn't just about pregnancy, of course, everyone will share ideas, knowledge, tips. You know Zorra is having terrible morning sickness and your ginger prepa-ration helped. She, and you, can talk about that."

"Oh." I take a careful breath. "Then, yes, of course I could attend and share information. I wasn't aware it was required."

"Well, nothing is mandated," she explains. "And right now, it's just an idea Bayla had to get pregnant humans together, for support and friendship. So many of them are a little lonely, so it's probably as much for company as anything else."

I am eager for time with friends, but this hardly seems the ideal solution. "I'd love that," I tell her, grinning in a way that shows my teeth and probably looks fake, but she's turned to another human who is hovering near us.

"Katrin! You look amazing. Your face positively glows."

Katin puts a hand on the small swell on her belly and beams. "I'm so happy." She literally does shine, and I wonder if something about being pregnant with a Zandian baby does something special to a human's anatomy, because I've never before seen a pregnant woman this beatific.

I offer my congratulations and hug her, and then I leave fast, eager to get back to my lab and finish my current work there.

When I get back, I head straight back to my lab space, instead of walking into the dome to greet my other mates. It's awful, but lately I simply can't bear looking them in the eyes, and I come up with more elaborate excuses every day to avoid their company. I have even been excusing myself from mating on occasion, saying that I have cramps or a headache. That, in turn, often results in a real headache when they fuss about me. Jax offers to take me to Dr. Daneth. Tarren complains that I work too hard. Then there is Ronan, trying to make me smile with a silly story. I'm sure they're all confused, and maybe even hurt, but sometimes I can't—I just can't. They trust me and care for me so much, and I can't keep up my deception much longer, and it's killing me. I'm terrified of what they'll say and do when they find out I've been lying, and that I accepted them as mates knowing I couldn't bear young. How can they forgive me for it?

Jax has already dropped a delivery pod in my lab, and it's waiting beside the door.

I wonder if it's seeds, or more books from Dr. Daneth. But when I peer through the glass, something disturbingly familiar catches my eye. I see a small, silver disc with Ocretion lettering. An info disc. This drives fear into my heart, because it's labeled:

"SLAVE 4356778A-CS-3. RIYA."

*O*h no. Fuck, no.

I put a hand to my mouth, and the nausea that's been hitting me more often pulses hard. I run outside and make it just in time to retch the contents of my stomach into the fragrant basil I've grown near our dome entrance. Even after my stomach is long empty, the convulsions continue until I'm dizzy and my throat is raw, and my eyes tear up. Finally I whimper and wipe my mouth on the back of my hand, and clean up with water. Moving mechanically, I dab my eyes and brush my sweaty hair out of the way.

A strange sense of calm envelops me. Of course it was bound to happen. King Zander said he'd send them back when he approved our homestead. Now that they're here, I simply must accept life as I know it is over.

As I stare at the piece of holographic aluminum, I can only see the faces of my mates, strong and beautiful. Ronan, so compact, his laugh lighting up his eyes, the way he makes it his whole goal to make me smile. Jax, insightful, the one who makes me think well of myself—not to mention his handsome face. And Tarren, my gruff warrior, the one who'd move the planets to ensure my comfort, the one who gets me in a deep way, making me feel like I'm not alone in this universe.

Then I think about the future, about how being with me ensures that all of their traits and wonders will die out. This is so much more than my own life and security. My selfishness has cost Zandia, but it's not too late to fix it. I need to let them be with another mate, and I need to do it in a way that ensures they'll never want me back.

I love them so deeply that I need to do this now, and fast, before I lose courage. I need to leave them in a way that is unforgivable, because my mates surely have forgiveness in them too.

After vomiting one more time, emptying myself of all the water I just drank, I pack a small satchel and grab my vest. Then I sit at the table and record the message. When I'm done, I carefully place the silver disc next to the comm device, and call Lily. My voice is even as I speak. "I need some help."

Tarren

I'm so eager to see Riya after my long planet rotation that I brush past Ronan and Jax, not caring if I'm rude, ready to show her what I've brought. My heart leaps with unaccustomed anxiety as I shift the package in my arms, hoping it will please her. Maybe even help her pop out of her current slump, which we all feel.

But Jax and Ronan don't accept my dominance.

Ronan elbows me. "Wait your turn, cousin." He's smiling, but the elbow hits my ribs, hard.

"Oof," I grunt, scowling. If I weren't holding this precious delivery of old Earth texts loaded onto holo comms, I'd drop him right now.

Taking advantage of our mini skirmish, Jax passes us both and enters the dome.

"Riya!" he calls, his voice jolly. Then—"Riya?"

Hearing the question in his voice, I spin away from Ronan and trot into the dome, dropping my package by the door. "What's going on?"

He frowns down at our group comm tablet, his back straight.

"What is that?"

"It's a message. From Riya." His voice is strange, flat.

"What did she say?" Ronan's eager tone falters. "Where is she?"

"She left." Jax is expressionless. He puts the comm unit down and walks to the window. "She's gone."

"To the forest again?"

Icy spires of anxiety curl through my chest as I grab the comm unit and play the message.

Jax, Ronan, Tarren, I need to leave. I'm sorry I'm not brave enough to say this to your faces, but it's time I was honest. This mating group won't work, and you will need to choose another mate.

I deceived you.

I can't have children.

I know how Zandians feel about lying, so I understand you will rightfully hate me. I don't know what King Zander will do with me, since I'm unable to breed, but I will throw myself at his mercy. Maybe he will even allow me to stay on Zandia. Either way, I hope—

Her voice breaks off, choked.

I hope you find a better female, one who will be able to commit to you fully and give you what you need and deserve.

"What the *veck*?" roars Ronan.

"She lied." My voice is dull even though my hands shake. All I can see is red.

"What does this even mean? She's infertile?" Ronan grabs his head. "*Vecking* tell me!"

Jax touches the disc. "Her records. Let's find out." He slides the thin silver disc into the comm port and documents flash up on the screen.

Slave determined to be incapable of fertilization. Slave notified of her physical condition. Slave understands that she can never become pregnant.

"*Veck*." Ronan's tone is low with disbelief. "It can't be right. It's the wrong report."

"It's not." Jax shakes his head. "It was labeled with her name and slave number. The barcode from her neck."

I grab the device back to read more.

"Has King Zander read it?" Ronan leans close to my face to see.

"I don't know what any being has *vecking* done." My frustration spills over and I stand up, needing to get away from his breath, his sweaty scent, his presence. Riya lied to us. She purposely deceived us all these lunar cycles.

It's so dishonorable. So un-Zandian. Of course, she's not a Zandian, she's a *vecking* human. And humans lie. How could we have trusted her? We trusted her with our *vecking hearts*!

"She's infertile. And she knew." Jax's voice is flat. "She knew about this and didn't tell us." He stares out the glass. "She let us wonder and worry about whether she was pregnant, and all along, she knew."

"I don't understand it. Why did she lie?" I can't make sense of it.

Jax shrugs. "She's afraid of being sent away. She lacks honor. Maybe she figured we'd never find out. Maybe she's just a *vecked* up human who makes cruel decisions. Or that we're not worth the truth. Who knows."

"Speak for yourself. I'm worth the truth." But Ronan's voice shakes.

I pick up the comm unit and scroll further.

The next headline is expected.

S LAVE 4356778A-CS-3 CONVICTED OF MURDER. SENTENCED TO DEATH.

"W e knew she was rescued from the death pod," Jax says, his voice eerily calm. "And that she killed a guard. Humans aren't sentenced to death unless it's a severe reason."

I grab at the comm unit. "She killed two guards." I read on. "Not one. It says she lashed out because they discovered her inability to breed and wanted to punish them for her own flaws. So she used gardening tools to slice their necks while they slept. They said that one of her psychological flaws is called *psychotic affect*. It's a human condition where a being lacks emotion and empathy. They said they don't want that in their breeding line."

"As angry as I am at her, they probably deserved it," Jax comments. Right now, he sounds devoid of any emotion.

"Regardless, it's a rash decision." Ronan's voice is hard. "Stupid. Slaves know they will be sentenced to death for taking a guard's life. Why would she risk it?"

None of us know the answer.

"I bet she's with Lily. We need to talk to Riya. I need to hear it from her." I tap wildly at my comm bracelet to initiate a call, but Jax grabs my wrist.

"Don't." He shakes his head. His purple skin has turned a pale lavender. "Do we want a deceitful mate? This is just like Gunt, all over again."

I stare at him, my heart in my damn boot.

It *is* like our former friend's deception, which dragged us into an investigation by King Zander, and could've had us banished to prison for life, like him.

"She made her choice. She's gone," Jax says.

"There's no place for lies between mates," Ronan says, equally pale.

I sink into the nearest hover chair, defeated. "No." My voice sounds hollow. "There isn't."

R onan

My *vecking* chest is ripped open. "We're better off without a liar."

"She's not loyal, like we are. She accepted our crystals!"

Tarren's anguish rings out. "You don't trick your way into that. Unless it meant nothing in the first place. Nothing but a way to hide out for a while, taking advantage of fools like me. Idiots who think they can—oh, *veck* it all."

The sun has set, and the darkness creeps in, insidious, like a fog. "Where do you think she is right now?"

No being answers me.

"What will we tell others?" My face burns with embarrassment. "*Veck*, everyone will know we picked an inferior mate!" Even as I say it, I can't believe it's true. Riya was perfect—so perfect. But it was all a lie.

"It's not our fault," Jax snaps, his cool finally broken. "She's the one. She is infertile, and she lied about it. And that's on top of being a murderer! With her, we could never father a child. Or have trust."

We're silent, I assume each Zandian thinking about this. To be honest, although I think young are cute, they are a little terrifying, and I never felt the driving need to have one of my own. I was excited more because it seemed a challenge, and because it's good for Zandia, and because... well, I thought Riya wanted it. But it wasn't even in my mind when I claimed her.

"She should have told us." Tarren's voice is loud. "Allowed us to decide if it mattered. Hiding it is a coward's way. We do not deserve a coward."

Something twists in my gut. Would it have mattered? If she'd told us from the start she couldn't conceive, would we have still chosen her?

A little voice in the back of my head screams *yes*.

But it's too late now. She lied, and she's gone. King Zander will decide her fate.

Veck.

"We deserve better, cousins." Jax rummages in a

cupboard and brings out a bottle of Oteera Spirits, imported at great cost and swaddled in layers of protective wrapping from the Oteraian Galaxy, on a planet known for their distilleries. "I was saving this for when Riya finally..." he pauses, looking ill. "But perhaps we should drink it now, because that other thing will never happen." He smiles, but it's mirthless, and when he pours us three tall glasses of the clear, powerful liquor, his fingers tremble.

I take a deep swallow, and the fluid burns like fire in my throat, the taste of juniper blasting my tongue, causing me to cough and splutter. "*Veck*. I haven't had this in a while."

Zandians don't need liquid nutrition, but alcohol affects our physiology in much the same way it does other beings, and I admit that sometimes we indulge. Rarely—because warriors can't be weak. This seems like an appropriate time, if there ever was one.

Tarren tosses his glass back without a sound, and Jax sips his, morose, tapping his long fingers in the table. We're silent for long minutes, until my vision softens, and the room seems warmer, brighter, as if the edges of everything are soft, like Riya's fleece blanket, the one that smells of her.

"Why would she be so duplicitous?" I say, enunciating to avoid slurring, an unfortunate side effect of spirits.

"Does it matter? She was, and is, and we're done with her. We're done!" Jax announces and pours himself a second glance. "She needs protection from beasts? Someone to plow her fields for her *vecking* calendula, over and over again? She can find... some other being."

Except I can see by Jax's face he doesn't believe what he's saying. Heartbreak is written all over it.

Tarren nods. "And when she gets lonely at night, she can find herself some other being to *veck*. We don't *veck* traitors."

That thought makes me clench my fists with rage. Riya with some other being?

Over my dead body. But she left.

"She betrayed us." My eyes burn.

"Cousin, hold up." Tarren puts his paw onto my shoulder, a rare gesture of affection. "We will find another mate, one who will... be... better. For us all." He drains his glass again. Jax quietly refills it.

"Beings will talk." I stare into my glass, where the liquid curls into oily swirls, a mouth that laughs.

"If anyone mocks us, I will *vecking* destroy them." Tarren slams his glass down. "We are not a laughingstock."

"No! We aren't!" I agree. The room tilts in a congenial way. "We're honorable. Powerful." I dig deep for an anger at Riya. "I'm glad she's gone. Good riddance."

Too bad I don't believe a *vecking* word of it.

12

Riya

I throw up three times on the flight home.

Lily shoots me worried glances from the cockpit, but I can't even speak to her. I don't want to tell her what's happened. The pain I just caused my dear, dear mates. It's too awful to discuss.

Tears spill down my face as I watch the landscape fly beneath us. I feel dead.

Fucking dead.

I don't even care what King Zander does to me. I don't care if he sends me back to the Ocretions to execute. Nothing matters without my mates.

But this will be better for them. I hope to our sweet Mother Earth and to the Zandian Star they will find a new mate. Happiness.

I know I never will.

J*ax*

I awake abruptly, my mouth dry, my head pounding. Then it floods back: *Riya*. Her betrayal. Her infertility. Getting drunk with my cousins. Tarren is on a side hover-seat. It's no surprise he didn't want to sleep in the usual disk, the one we and Riya typically share. *Shared*. Ronan is passed out in the corner, not even on a disk or mattress. He's going to have one hell of a hangover in the morning.

I lie awake, trying to figure out what's tugging at my mind. I'm so angry at Riya I can barely think, but there is something I need to do, something important—

The records. It occurs to me that we never read them all. Surely there must be more information there? I can't sleep, so I head back to the main area and turn on the comms device, reading everything in order, now, not just the first things we saw.

Scans and data flash in front of my eyes, and the burn in my heart intensifies, seeing the woman I loved reduced to a set of numbers. Date of birth. Size: height, weight, all measurements, done several times annually. Genetic analysis and psych profiling to determine whether she was worthy of breeding, and if so, with whom, to ensure a stronger slave for future Ocretion usage.

As it turned out, I read, her Ocretion captors determined her unworthy of future breeding, as she had "defects" that made her "unviable" for future slave generations. One of them was her intellect. Human slaves were desired to be smart, but not too smart; this line that the Ocretions were creating was to be a hard-working ag force who took orders well and didn't question authority. Riya asked too many questions. Sometimes argued too much. Was far too clever.

As such, she was tagged as a "secondary" at a young age. Bile crawls up my throat. Everyone knows that to an Ocretion, a secondary human slave is considered one step above trash. They don't eliminate secondaries, because they are still valuable workers while they live. But in reality, secondaries are often turned into rape toys for the psychotic, cruel guards, and expected to continue working hard without sympathy, sometimes even harder than their primary peers, who are treated more kindly—at least, until they provide a sufficient number of new slaves to be trained. At that point, once they are past breeding age, the primaries are usually demoted to secondary as well.

The rage at this overtakes me and I curse, slamming my fist onto the table. This is why Zander outlawed slavery. It is simply wrong on every level. *Veck*, no being deserves to be treated like this. Even if I'm mad at Riya right now, beyond angry—this makes me ill. I wish we had the power to kill every *vecking* Ocretion right now and free every enslaved being in the galaxy, and I vow to someday be a part of that effort, no matter what it takes. But first, Zandia. We cannot do more to help the galaxy until we first strengthen ourselves into a super power.

Riya. Oh, Riya.

Something catches my eye, and I scroll past more annual reports to something that stands out. Something that has me back in the sleep area, tugging at my cousins.

"Ronan. Tarren. Get the *veck* up. I need you to see this."

It's a slow process, like a towship tugging a disabled galactacarrier, but I persist, and the two of them stagger out, rubbing their eyes, haggard.

"I need you two to read this." I point at the comms

device. They blink, so I paraphrase what I learned. "It says that due to chronic electro-stimulation, Ocretion physicians have determined that structural changes occurred in her uterus, rendering her permanently incapable of achieving fertilization." When they just look at me, uncomprehending, I scowl. "Don't you get it? *Chronic electro-stimulation* is a pretty way of saying *torture with their shock sticks.*"

"Wait." Ronan frowns, grabs my arm, his fingers digging in, and stares at the screen. "The reason she can't get pregnant is because they tortured her?"

"I will kill them all." Tarren's voice is so cold that I know he'd do it, if he could.

"It appears so," I answer Ronan—Tarren's comment requires no reply. "I knew they used shock sticks on her. She told us. But I had no idea..." my voice cracks. "That it was done like this, or so extensively as to damage her."

"Let me see the names." Tarren's hand darts out and he grabs the comm. "Look at this. Jax, Ronan." He gets louder. "The two guards who were on her daily duty, they were the ones she killed. And the data doesn't match. They said she snuck out at night in the judicial report, but here, this report says they died in an altercation in her sleep quarters. The altercation was between her, a younger slave, and the two guards. They were probably torturing her, and she lashed out to protect herself."

"Or she was protecting the younger slave." My stomach turns. "How much evil exists in this universe?"

"I don't know, but maybe... perhaps we were too hasty with our angry words last night." I bite my lip.

"She left us," Tarren corrects, but his voice rises, as if on a question. "And she deceived us."

"She did." I agree. "But maybe... there was more to it than what it seems."

"Maybe..." Tarren pauses.

"Maybe what?" I'm eager, snatching at his words. "What?" It will only make sense if someone else thinks it, too.

"Don't rush me." He scowls and runs a hand over his face. "Is there water?" He finds a pitcher and drinks to counteract the alcohol. "What if it was more complicated, like you said."

"How so?" Ronan grabs the water from his hand and splashes some on his face.

"Use a *vecking* towel!" thunders Tarren, wiping droplets from his arm with a grimace. "Are you a toddler?" He sits down. "What if she's more broken than we knew?"

"She was more broken. She can't bear young," Ronan points out.

"Not like that. Inside her soul." Tarren thumps his chest. "And don't *vecking* laugh at me," he orders, piercing us both with his dark eyes. Neither of us move. He continues, "I'm not good at this. But what if she chose to leave first because she thought we'd throw her out?"

I blink, a seed of hope starting to grow. "That's what I'm beginning to wonder."

"If she knew she couldn't have young, and there's a bounty on her head for murder, surely she was worried for her very life?" Tarren's voice gains strength.

"What," scoffs Ronan. "Like we'd toss her back to the Ocretians if we found out?"

The words hang in the air like a poisonous gas.

"Maybe," I say eventually. "Perhaps she did wonder about it. After all, King Zander never made any mention of what might happen if a human couldn't bear children."

"What would happen?" Tarren furls his brow. "Would

he... force her to leave her mates so a new human could try?" He wrinkles his nose. "That's unpalatable."

"But perhaps necessary, from a lineage perspective," I point out, although something in me protests at the thought.

"But does that even make sense? After all, there are still many more males than females," argues Ronan. "It's impossible that all of us could father a child right now. There simply aren't enough human females to go around. There are still many unmated Zandian males at this point, even if they team up in groups of three and four. So..."

We are silent again, this time longer.

"I don't care," Tarren says, and stands up. "I want her anyway. Even if she never can give me young." He has that stubborn face I recognize, the one he wears into battle, the expression that inspires us all. Because when his visage is this strong and set, there is no chance we can lose. "I love her, and I can forgive her for what she did. And if you two are the Zandians I think you are, you'll agree."

I get up, and stand beside him, as if we are readying ourselves for war. "I am with you."

Veck, I hope it's not too late. What if King Zander has already sentenced her to some horrible punishment for her deceit? Or—*star forbid*—sent her away? And we weren't there to defend her? To protect her? To vouch for her?

I grind my teeth and tighten my fingers into fists. It's unconscionable.

Ronan hesitates, and I see his youth in his eyes, and a hurt he can't hide. His emotions are on easy display.

"Cousin," I tell him softly, although I stay next to Tarren. "If we are right, she only lied because she was afraid."

He still doesn't get up, and I hold my breath. We can't even try unless all three of us are on board. Finally he gets to his feet and comes toward us, extending both hands. We each take one and squeeze.

Tarren smiles. "We will go to King Zander and tell him that we demand to have her back," he orders. "That we do not care about young, although they are fine for others who desire them and can handle their annoying habits. Of course."

"Yes," I say, my heart exulting. "We will tell her that we mated her, and that bond can stretch, and it encompasses forgiveness and tolerance. Understanding. Compromise. She does not need to leave."

"Cousins. Brothers," Ronan says. "Let's go get our mate."

13

Riya

I can't eat. I've just been hiding in Lily's chamber, with my head under the covers, crying since I arrived the planet rotation before.

Lily tries to soothe me. She keeps popping in, offering teas of chamomile and lemon balm, and those I accept. I'm staying under her guardianship right now in the palatial pod, until I'm granted an audience with Zander at his weekly open throne. It's an awkward situation at best, at least I haven't been summoned for immediate sentencing. That makes me think Zander won't banish me outright.

I betrayed him and my mates and have wasted valuable time by allowing them to all think I could become pregnant. If they'd been with another human, she'd probably be several lunar cycles into a pregnancy by now, and that would be one more Zandian baby to build our future.

I try to occupy my mind with my research. The books Dr. Daneth gave me contain calculus—something called differential equations. They make sense to me, the symbols dancing into my brain and locking into place, opening new corridors I should be eager to explore. My fingers attack the screen, tapping and clicking, moving the numbers around. I am the master here, in complete control. My brain lights up and my fingers move faster, as I figure something out. This is what I need to do, to figure out the right ratios for my latest—

"Riya?" Lily comes in with a tray of soup. "I have cream of mushroom—your favorite."

I retch at the smell. "Please take it away." I put a hand to my mouth as I look up from my screen. My voice is sharp, and I add, "I'm sorry, I'm just too upset to eat." Part of my irritation was not just at the intrusive odor, but the interruption to my trance. Now I'm back in reality, a place that is ugly for me, right now.

She nods and leaves, coming back empty handed. "You need sustenance, though."

"Maybe." I shrug. "If King Zander is going to send me away, it doesn't much matter, though."

Her expression drops. "He wouldn't do that."

I bite my lip. "I hope not. But it's his choice." A wave of dizziness rolls over me, and then another one, and I list in my chair, heart racing.

"Riya!" Lily is at my side in an instant. "You're not well. I'm calling Bayla." Bayla, Dr. Daneth's mate, was a breeding slave before Daneth bought her. She's works as his nurse now.

"Don't." I pull at her arm. "King Zander won't want you wasting resources on a traitor like me."

"You're not a traitor. You just... made a mistake." Her voice is hesitant, and I hear the conflict.

"It wasn't a mistake." At least I can be honest now. "It was a calculated decision. I chose not to tell them."

She grimaces. "Can you phrase it another way, when you talk to the king?"

"I'm done lying." I look at my tablet, but now my brain is too roiled up to focus. "It feels better to say things that are true. It's like tearing off a scab. It hurts, but it feels so good to reveal the skin beneath it."

"Riya." She sits beside me. "Please let me help."

"But you can't." I look at her, tears rising in my eyes. "If you can't heal me, you can't help me. It's that simple. Besides, I made my own choices, bad as they are, and I need to stand behind that."

"Your worth is not solely placed on your womb," she snaps, suddenly mad. She touches my stomach. "Men are not judged solely by their ability to procreate. There are other ways to contribute to society. It would be a very foolish leader who does not understand that and allow for options. How can you not see that? Do you think Zander to be such a simpleton?"

"No! I don't. I think he's a leader who's looking out for what's best for his planet and his people and having a lying criminal may not be the right thing. I've tried. Mother Earth, how I've tried to make myself useful these past lunar cycles."

"And you are," she insists. "Don't you see how your creations are valued? Dr. Daneth even said your salicylic acid idea may revolutionize the future of topical pain medicine for not just Zandians, but other species as well."

My pride flashes but is doused. "But is that enough to make me worth keeping?"

"What if you were just a regular human without special skills, wouldn't that make you worth keeping?" She touches my knee. "You helped in battle, you won your freedom, now you're here. You're part of this land. It's impossible to assume that every single human will be able to have young. It's not logical. You can't just toss out people."

Bayla enters the chamber. "Riya, Lily." She nods.

I raise my hand. "Hello."

"I hear you're not well? You don't look well." She glances at me, her gaze lingering on my belly, and I flinch, as if my barren status shows in my very skin. "Come with me, to Dr. Daneth's lab for an examination."

I'm about to protest, but Dr. Daneth enters. His eyes are cool and assessing as he looks at me. "Come. I must examine you, Riya." It sounds more like an order than a request.

I get up and follow them to Dr. Daneth's examination room. Lily shoots me a sympathetic look as I leave.

Dr. Daneth attaches a soft silver clip to my finger and records some data. "Remove your clothing," he says, his voice distant. "I need to attach these." He holds up electrodes, and I comply, numb, as he attaches leads, takes an EKG. He grabs a blood sample with a small silver device. Nothing hurts, but I don't know what they're going to do with this data. Add it to my file, maybe.

Bayla presses my body, my lymph nodes, and when she reaches my belly, I recoil. "Ugh."

"Does that hurt?" She and the doctor exchange a glance.

"I'm just upset," I say. "And there's a pain here." I point to my lower abdomen. "Probably from not eating."

"Is it sharp or dull?" she asks, pressing again. "Here?"

"Ow. Yes. Sharp, sometimes."

Dr. Daneth repeats it, his fingers precise, locating the exact spot. "Interesting."

"How so?" I ask, but he doesn't answer, as he's busy typing something into his screen.

"I'm going to run a scan," he says. "Bayla, will you bring me the hand sono?"

His mate provides a small, handheld scanner, and he presses it to my belly. "You may have a benign cyst," he explains. "If you do, it is easily treated."

He presses a button and the device beeps. It's something I've used as a medic; sometimes we needed to assess the deep tissue damage to know if there were nicks to internal organs before providing attention. I never expected one to be used on me.

The machine beeps again. "Interesting," he repeats, and frowns.

My brain is so numb I don't even care to ask what is so interesting. I assume he will tell me, in due time.

"Why don't you get dressed," he says slowly, and tilts his head at Bayla. "I'm going to go process this and then I'll come back to discuss your exam."

"Thank you." The words are ridiculous, and after they leave the room, I pull on my clothes and stand up, and cross my arms, trying not to feel too much like a prisoner awaiting sentence. What could be worse than a lying criminal? A lying criminal who can't have babies, and on top of that is ill, needing special attention from the doctor and nurse, who have much better things to do.

Mother Earth. Yes, cysts are not that complicated to handle. But I've already caused enough trouble.

While I'm waiting, King Zander, himself, enters.

I jump down from the examination table where I've perched and curtsy. I didn't expect to see him here. My heart pounds, wondering if he's decided what to do with me.

"Are you well?" he asks, his gaze probing.

"Well enough to talk to you, my lord," I reply. "And apologize. I am sorry that I was not honest about my reproductive status. I knew I could not have young, and yet I allowed —I mated Tarren, Jax, and Ronan. And I didn't tell them, either." I swallow hard. "It was wrong. I hope I have done enough good for the planet that I may stay and help where I can."

He gazes at me. "What did you think I would do?"

I shake my head. "Send me away to Jesel? Or another place? I don't know. I thought maybe you wouldn't want me here. I don't think I deserve to be sent back to the Ocretions. They will kill me." My voice falters.

King Zander sighs. "I have failed."

"No! Nothing I did was your fault." Terror rises; I'm sure he's going to say he failed by not recognizing my flaws, by allowing me to enter the program as a mate.

"I have failed in that I was not clear. The program started so quickly, and we did not think through all of the possible repercussions and possibilities."

"I don't understand."

"Riya, I would not have sent you away for being barren." His voice is patient. "As a freed slave, we owe you a life here. And that is true regardless of whether you can bear young."

My mouth drops open. "But you gave the speech about us being pioneers, making sacrifices. That we were the ones who would repopulate."

"All of that is true. But not every single individual will be able to participate in the exact same way. There will be some females who can't bear young. There may be some Zandians who do not choose to or cannot mate. They can help in other ways, as you suggested. We started the program so fast, with so much exuberance, but not every detail was worked out. In the future, I will undertake to fix the gaps. No, I would not have sent you away for that."

There's a "but" in his voice that chills me. "But you'll send me away for... lying? Deception?"

"Deception has no place here," he says, his voice firm. "It is a cancer to a new population that needs to trust each other to grow."

"So... where am I going, then?" I thought I didn't care, but I do. My eyes water and panic grips me. "If you give me another chance, I swear I will never be dishonest again. I will dedicate my life to helping this planet survive."

"I will probably remand you to your mates for punishment," he says mildly. "If they wish to keep you."

I nearly burst into tears then, because I know my mates won't want me back. They hate liars. They made that perfectly clear numerous times.

The door glides open, and there are my mates: Tarren, Jax, and Ronan. I don't know who's more surprised, me or King Zander, but Tarren advances, his eyes glittering and roars, "She's not going anywhere. By the one true star, I swear, if you try to hurt her or send her away from Zandia, I will..."

"You will stop right now." King Zander puts up his hand, and Tarren growls, but stops in his tracks, breathing hard, Jax and Ronan flanking him. All three of my mates have expressions of determination on their faces, and I'm so happy to see them that I almost want to fly. Except that they'll never forgive me for my deception. "I am not sending her away. I was never going to do that. We are merely having a discussion about honesty and trust."

"There are things you don't know about her," says Jax, his voice patient but firm and I see an iron will in him that matches the strength of Tarren. "She has been through unspeakable things, and we forgive her for lying to us."

"You do?" I'm so shocked I stare at him, mouth open.

"Yes." Ronan smiles at me. "Yes, we're angry that you lied for so long. But we think we understand why you did it. We forgive you and want you to come back with us."

"But I can't have young. You three, you can't waste yourselves on me." My voice is as weak as I feel. I can't hear this right now. I'm going to give in, and that was the thing I swore I wouldn't do. They deserve better than this.

"We don't care," announces Tarren, and everyone in the room reacts. Lily, who peeks in, with Dr. Daneth and the midwife at her heels, squeaks. Tarren continues. "It's not a *waste*. Riya, you're strong and smart and fun. Being with you makes us happier and stronger. It makes me enjoy life in a way I never did. I won't get that with another mate, and I don't want it with another. I want it with you. With or without young."

Bayla clears her throat. "Ah, it turns out that Dr. Daneth has to tell you something important..."

Jax acts like she hasn't spoken as he stares into my eyes. "You give us more energy to be successful at our jobs. Your advice helps us thrive and make better decisions. Your love and adventurous spirit during sex..." my cheeks redden, and I dart a glance at Lily and King Zander, before looking back to Jax, "makes us *vecking* enjoy life again."

All three of them chuckle, and even King Zander stifles a grin.

Ronan pipes up. "Laughing with you, and making you laugh, lightening your worries, makes me feel useful. Then I'm stronger and more confident in my daily activities, knowing you rely on me. You're so much more than just... this." He presses his belly. "Besides, young are smelly and irritating. They are such a bother with their disgusting diapers all the time, and the incessant squalling. We will never have to worry about that. See, it might even be a benefit."

"Um, Riya, I really think you need to let Dr. Daneth tell you—" Bayla starts.

"Young are dreadful," agreed Tarren. "I shudder every time I see one." He darts an apologetic look at Bayla. "I scare them with my face and never know what to say to one. And how do you even hold one without cracking it in half? The whole thing is a nightmare." He shakes his head. "Besides, Ronan is so immature sometimes that he's like a young. You will get the experience anyway."

"*Veck* you, cousin," Ronan starts, and Jax holds him back, smiling.

I laugh and cry at the same time, holding a hand to my mouth. "But no. You can't. You are so strong and amazing. You need a better mate, someone who can give you..."

"No one is better for us than you," snaps Tarren. "We've already bonded. You wear our crystals. That connection doesn't tear lightly, Riya. Look into your heart. Is that bond gone? I think it's still here, as strong as ever." He stares at me.

"I just want..." I falter. "I want to do the right thing."

"But there is no one right thing. We must all determine what's right for us." He touches my arm.

King Zander clears his throat. "Are you saying that the four of you want to continue on as a mated team?"

"Yes!" say all my Zandians at once.

"Riya?" King Zander looks at me.

"You'll allow that? I can't believe it. Yes. I do, more than anything!"

Zander nods. "In the future, you must not deceive me, or your mates again. And you should not make assumptions about what I will or will not do. Assumptions are dangerous and have started many civilizations on the road to failure. But yes, you have bonded with these three Zandians, and that is sacred. Once they punish you for your deceit and have forgiven you, then you may move on. Nobody said this would be easy. None of us should give up at the first hurdle. We are made of stronger stuff than that, human and Zandians both. If our planet cannot handle some fights and disagreements, some compromise, then we are doomed." He smiles. "And we are not doomed. We are going to succeed."

He adds, "And I own a part of improving the process for the future. I should have anticipated that humans would have worries and concerns like yours. I will ensure that there are guidelines in place that clarify."

Dr. Daneth speaks up. "It turns out that human emotions are far more volatile than I could have predicted," he says, "even with my best research. They often make rash decisions when angry or hurt and are rather unpredictable in group mating situations. We will need to... adjust our protocols accordingly. Change our training." He gives me a look that is probably as close to sympathetic as he is capable of providing. "Perhaps we need to look into past histories more closely ahead of time, and work with each human to discuss potential problems and pitfalls."

"I told you," Ronan says to Jax and Tarren, a touch of superiority in his voice, "that it would be fine with King Zander. After all, there are far more Zandian men than humans. It is not a problem if the three of us do not have young."

"Actually," Bayla interrupts again. "About that."

"What is it?" Jax turns to her.

"Well, it's very interesting, because, Dr. Daneth has discovered that..."

"That what?" I blink. "Am I dying? What is it? Just say it." I turn to the physician. "Dr. Daneth?"

He nods. "You're six weeks pregnant."

"I'm what?" My head spins. "Don't mock me."

"It's no joke." His voice is stiff. "Do not disrespect my profession by insinuating I would joke about something so critical. Your blood test shows an increase in HCG and your sonogram shows a healthy embryo with a heartbeat. Actually, two embryos. Twins. I did not tell you immediately when I saw it, because I wanted to verify they are healthy and well-formed by analyzing the data further. They are. Healthy and normal, that's it."

"I'm sorry, I mean no disrespect, but I can't... this can't be. You saw my reports, what they did to me. My fallopian tubes were fused shut, destroyed. It's not possible. Right? Or was it something else?" I find a chair and sit, head swimming, and my mates surround me, their hands warm on my face, my arms, my hands. I squeeze and lean back, so grateful they are here.

"Maybe the Zandian sperm helped heal you," Bayla suggests. "Or the planetary crystal. But right now, we don't have a medical reason why your body would heal itself. It's a novel phenomenon."

I still can't process this. "I'm really pregnant? For real?"

She nods. "That is why you are so sick," she says. "Some women have very serious morning sickness; in your case, it's severe. But I had a suspicion you were pregnant, based on the smell of your breath."

"The smell of my breath?" I can't comprehend this.

She nods. "It's a very subtle thing that sometimes happens when humans are pregnant with non-human babies—their breath smells like apples. When we examined you... it became clear."

I remembered Holla had mentioned my breath smelling like apples, too. Had she suspected?

"But... *twins*?" It's boggling my mind.

Dr. Daneth interrupts. "I would like to research the breath situation," he says. "I would like to get samples of Riya's exhalations and run them through a CG to check which volatile compounds are responsible for the odor. It could be a useful addition to our diagnostic arsenal." He coughs. "I still have much to learn about humans," he admits.

Bayla adds, "You will need to stay on bedrest until the pain resolves and you regain enough weight. We need to be very careful. We don't know why your tubes reopened, Riya, but you are still fragile. We need to treat your pregnancy very carefully, especially with twins."

"The bigger one is probably mine," says Ronan, touching my still-flat belly. "I bet mine will be huge."

"Don't be ridiculous," snaps Tarren. "They are both from the same Zandian. And the bigger one would be mine, anyway." He puts his large hand over mine and squeezes. "And we will care for them regardless." He gives me a guilty look. "We only said those things because we thought you couldn't have one. Of course we, ah, are now very excited about this." He's nervous; I can tell from the way he shifts his leg and taps his foot. But something in his eyes shows deep excitement, too. He's getting something he never though he could or should. A gift.

"We would have been more than satisfied without young," Jax explains. "But this is clearly important to you, and I'm delighted. Either way we want you, Riya." He caresses my head, massaging my scalp with his fingers, a soothing feeling.

"Have I told you how much I want young?" Ronan says.

"So amazing! Remarkable creatures. I can't wait to, ah, change diapers for you." He blanches so that even his horns get paler, and I laugh so hard I gag, but I grasp his hand on my belly.

"I'm sure you will become an expert very quickly," I tell him with a smile.

"We are going to start you on an IV infusion of vitamins and anti-nausea meds," says Dr. Daneth. "And soon we expect you'll be able to eat again and regain your strength." He adds, "They could be identical twins, or fraternal. And I have to tell you that there is a chance they could be from two different fathers, if you both... penetrated her... in short succession, and she released two eggs. We won't know until we do genetic testing, but I don't recommend that until she regains strength."

I don't even care about that right now. All I can focus on is having my mates here. Tarren, Ronan, and Jax have forgiven me. They came for me. They want me, after everything that happened. It's incredible.

"When can we take her home?" Tarren asks, and it sounds more like a demand.

"She'll need to stay in a medbay for now," the doctor answers. "Until we can get her weight up and assess the safety of the pregnancy. It may be just a few planet rotations, or possibly a few lunar cycles."

"Then we will live in the pod with her," declares Ronan. "And go to work from there. It will be smaller than the dome, but we will make it work."

"You will do no such thing," advises the doctor, rolling his eyes. "The pod room she will be in is for one patient only, but you may, of course, visit daily." He eyes my mates with narrowed eyes, as if he doesn't trust them to listen.

"You truly want me?" I need to hear it again, and again.

"Yes," they all say, their voices blending into a symphony of tones, my favorite sounds in the world.

"I love you," I whisper, looking at each one in turn. And it's true. I love these Zandians as much as I love life itself. I touch my belly, and feel the most incredible joy possible, knowing that my past is truly in the past. Despite my mistakes, even after everything that happened, my future is bright and beautiful... full of everything I could have dreamed.

14

Tarren

"Do you need more tea?" I hover over Riya, placing the soft fleece throw she likes over her lap. "Stay warm."

She tosses it off. "Tarren, it's like a hundred degrees in here, and with Zandian twins in my belly, my temperature is twice that." She makes a face at me and laughs. Now that she's past the morning sickness, color has returned to her face, and she's glowing. To me, she's never looked more lovely.

I grab her and pull her to her feet and kiss her, reaching back to smack her ass. "Don't talk back, human," I admonish her.

"Ow!" she whines, but then she sticks her ass out, as if asking for another swat. "You don't have to punish me." She stands on tiptoe to bite my neck, and then reaches up to squeeze my horns. "Unless you really want to."

Jax comes up and cups her ass in his hands as she grinds up against my hips. "Dr. Daneth did give her all-clear for full activities," he says. "And he did mean... full." He raises his eyebrows. "Apparently, spanking a human during a Zandian pregnancy causes no harm at all, and the increased blood flow from orgasms is good for fetal development. And King Zander *did* say you required punishment."

"Yes, he did," I murmur, flicking her left nipple. She squeaks and pushes back into Jax. "Then we should probably be sure to punish her and *veck* her well... if it's good for the babies."

"We definitely need to take care of the babies, starting now," agrees Ronan, stripping his shirt, his bare chest shining in the light. "Riya, get naked for us, so we can give you a good spanking."

"It's time to punish her for leaving us," I say, making sure that my tone of voice shows affection.

"I came back, though," she reminds me, reaching down to stroke my cock.

"True," I admit. "But only because we came after you. If we hadn't..."

"I said I was sorry." She moans as I bite her neck in the place she loves.

"And now you can show us just how much," I say, matter of factly. "Don't you think that's a good plan?"

By the scent of her arousal, I can tell that she does like the plan very much, but she protests anyway. "Don't use the whip."

"Mmm..." I pretend to think it over. "Probably just the strap and paddle, and an ass plug or two. And we'll see if you need more after that."

Her scent gets stronger, as it always does at the threats I make. Our human *vecking* loves playing rough with us.

"I might need more," she murmurs, reaching up to rub my horns again. "I really was very disobedient, after all."

"You were, and right now you're making it far worse. Ronan gave you a command," I remind her, narrowing my eyes and acting stern, trying not to pant and just toss her on the hoverdisk. "Are you naked yet, beautiful?"

She steps back and looks at herself in surprise. "Oh! I guess I'm not, am I? Well, I suppose I'll have to take care of that." She looks at each of us in turn and shoots a mischievous grin at me. "Watch carefully to make sure I don't miss anything, please."

She turns her back to us and drops the straps of her gown, revealing her creamy shoulders, and I catch my breath, cock twitching. Jax groans, and Ronan growls, "*Veck*," as the gown falls, her gorgeous ass on full display.

"You're not wearing panties?" I demand, my eyebrows shooting up. "*Veck*, Riya."

"They're too hot," she murmurs, turning around. "Besides, don't you like having easier access?"

Her breasts have become even fuller these past weeks, and her nipples, ruddy and large, stand at attention. The soft swell of her belly inflames me further, knowing I did that.

These breasts need to be bitten," I growl, striding towards her. "They're perfectly red and ripe for my mouth." I don't waste time with more words, but close my lips around the left one, sucking and teasing with my tongue, until she squeals and grabs my hair, hard, yanking it.

"Tarren," she gasps. "So good."

I pop my mouth from her nub. "Who will be first to enjoy her pussy? Spread your legs, Riya, and keep them wide for your mates."

"I volunteer," Ronan says, and is there in a flash kneeling between her thighs, which he spreads wider by tapping her foot and adjusting her stance.

She shifts, and I can tell the moment that Ronan puts his tongue to her flesh, because she moans into me and jerks a little, as I continue to lick her nipples. Her body is so responsive, in pregnancy even more than before, and we enjoy teasing her and getting her desperate and needy before we let her come.

It's only seconds before Ronan exclaims, "*Veck*, Riya, you're so wet and creamy. I could lick you for hours. If human food tasted of your pussy, I swear, by the one true star, I'd eat every planet rotation."

Riya makes a strangled sound, a combination of a laugh and moan of pleasure, because Ronan's head goes back between her thighs. Then she lets her head fall back, murmuring little sounds of enjoyment, and I see her pulse beat in her neck, fast and strong.

"Come, Riya," urges Ronan. "The first of a dozen, and I claim this one for me. Come on my tongue and shatter for me. Show me who owns you." His voice is hoarse with desire.

Riya's response is immediate. She cries out and stiffens, her whole body quivering, as she squeezes her eyes shut. I support her in my arms, watching in amazement as a fine sweat grows on her brow, loving the expressions she makes in her pleasure. It is a treat to watch her let go like this. I watch her peak and then slowly come down, her eyelids fluttering, murmuring little sounds, a smile on her face.

"Ronan," she breathes.

"I'm here." He comes out from her thighs. "And now I'd like you to return the pleasure, Riya."

I bite her neck and mutter, "And then you'll pleasure me next. This time I'm not *vecking* waiting for last." I can barely hold out as it is—just hearing the sound of my mate receiving pleasure is enough to make me explode. I take a breath. "Go please Ronan while Jax whips your ass for your disobedience." I can't for the *vecking* life of me remember what she did wrong, nor do I care. I just want to see her ass turn red, hear her cry out with those little breathy murmurs and whimpers as we stripe her and make her wet and needy.

She's still shaky from her orgasm, so I scoop her up in my arms and carry her to the sleep disc. "How do you want her, cousin?"

R *onan*

R iya's taste is on my lips, the sweet honey of her orgasm driving me insane. *Veck,* how I love making her fly apart with my mouth and my fingers. But now I want to drive into her body and take her hard.

"I want to sink my cock into your sweet pussy," I say, grasping my member and squeezing, a mix of pain and pleasure the sweetest anticipation. "Tarren, arrange her on her back, legs spread. Wide."

She doesn't need assistance—she opens her thighs and shoots me a smile. "Like this?" she reaches down to stroke her lips. "I'm still tingling. It's so good."

"You're going to come again before I'm through with you," I threaten, and she reaches out to stroke me as I kneel over her.

"I certainly hope so," she murmurs, winding her fingers around me and rubbing the way I love.

"Jax can punish you later," I add, because if I don't get

into her immediately, I won't last. I reach down and slap her outer thigh, once and again, to make her squeal and moan —a few spanks I can do. "And I'm sure he'll do a good job. Maybe you can think about that while I *veck* you, Riya. I'm letting you have your pleasure now, but you'll pay later."

Of course, the way we make her *pay* ends in pleasure for all, and at my words she arches her hips on the hoverdisk and gasps, her eyes going wide with lust and need. "Ronan."

"Wrap your legs around me as I enter you," I urge her, "and grab my horns. *Veck* me back, Riya. Fight me for the pleasure. Take it from me."

I'm lost in sensation as I drive into her wet heat. She's always so tight, her body fitting me to perfection, and there's no better feeling in the universe than this.

Just as I asked, my mate wiggles and squirms against me, pushing her hips up into me, working as hard as I do, arching and pulling to meet my body every time I thrust. There's something incredible about a mate who loves this like I do, who gets so *vecking* lost in her own pleasure that she uses me like a toy to tip off her cliff of passion.

The sensation of her fingers stroking and pulling my horns is delicious, and within seconds I feel my balls tighten and tingle with the inevitable urge to come, but I force myself to wait. "Riya. You don't get to come until I tell you."

"Oh, please!" she loves being told to wait, but right now she's as on edge as I. Luckily for her, I won't drag it out too long.

I slow my thrusts, tantalizing her with my cock, letting it brush her clit each time I pull out, until she squeezes her eyes shut and pants, making little moans—that means she's about to come. The sight of that alone makes me explode. "Come again for me, Riya," I demand, and she immediately cries out and arches into me with all of her strength, and I feel her pussy clench around my cock as I release into her, pure bliss suffusing my entire body.

J*ax*

Riya's ready for me, now—after relaxing in Ronan's arms, and refreshing herself in the shower, Tarren took her ass. Now she's lying on the hoverdisk, naked. And she shows no signs of exhaustion. I'd never want to push her while she's pregnant, but lately she's insatiable. Who knew it would take three of us to satisfy one human female? *Veck,* I can't imagine doing it alone.

Right now, though, alone is what I want—my turn alone with Riya. I lock eyes with her and smile, then look at the box. "What do you think I should use on you, Riya?"

She licks her lips, a flash of pink that drives my cock to get harder. "I..."

"I'm partial to the strap, as you know." I bend down and pick it up. I slap it against my palm, and she starts at the crack. I toss it to the hoverdisk and pick up a new little crop, a thin whippy strip of leather that Dr. Daneth said has proven highly effective in field studies. I didn't smile at all, even though I suspected that his *field study* was a *monumental sex session* with his mate, Bayla. I merely nodded and accepted the offering, telling him I'd try it out as soon as possible. Which is right now.

"And there's this," I add, swishing the little crop in the air. It makes a satisfying hiss, and I like the way her eyes widen. "It's supposed to sting quite a bit," I explain, testing it on my arm once, and again, to practice. "Oh, it does." I raise my eyebrows.

"I can't wait to see you stripe her ass with that," remarks Ronan, relaxed, on the side hoverdisk. He's the picture of lazy rest, but his eyes are alert and bright. "Turn her pink for us, Jax, so we can *veck* her again later and enjoy the heat and marks on her skin."

She moans at those words and I know she's getting wetter. She loves what we do to her, which is a *vecking* blessing from the stars.

"Lean over the hoverdisk," I order her. "Ass out, nice and high. Present yourself to me, Riya."

She scrambles to obey, getting in the wide-legged stance I like without needing to be asked, and I smile at the way she rushes to please me. "Is this wide enough?" she asks, darting a look over her shoulder, but then she licks her lips deliberately and smiles.

I growl. "Don't tease me, Riya, or I'll have to whip you harder for it."

Veck. I could spend just from that expression in her eye.

I stand at her side and run my hand down her back, the skin impossibly soft and pale, until I reach her ass. "So soft and pale," I remark. "For now."

She shudders under my touch, and I rub between her thighs, soft touches designed to tantalize. "Do you want my cock, Riya? Tell me."

"Yes, I want it, Jax, I do." she gasps as I press my finger deeper into her core, finding the spot that drives her wild. "Oh!"

She undulates her hips as I stroke. "Mmm..."

"Stand still," I whisper, pressing one hand into the small

of her back, and bend over to speak into her small, perfect ear. "Don't move your hips one inch. Let me touch you and tease you until I decide you're ready."

"Yes, Master," she whispers back, the tension already sounding in her tone. I can tell from the way she clenches her thighs that she's very needy, but she's obedient, our little mate. She takes a deep breath and stills her hips as I stroke and flick her clit.

"I'm not sure you're wet enough," I remark. "Let's see if this can help." I raise the crop and bring it down hard across both of her pert ass cheeks.

"Ouch!" She squeals and jumps, one hand darting back. "Jax, that's insane!"

All three of us stare at the thin red line across her pale skin, and I know I'm not the only one who finds this *vecking* hot.

"Hands down," I murmur, taking her palm and squeezing it, then arranging it back above her head. "You know the rules. Are you supposed to interfere with a punishment?"

"No, but that's wicked," she complains, twitching her hips.

"Mmm," I say, tracing the thin welt, making her hiss. "Just as wicked as you were. Shall we say, ten to start?"

"I think fifteen," says Tarren, from his hoverdisk, watching intently. "Five for each of us, just to remind her that she's ours."

"I agree," Ronan adds. "Nice hard ones, too."

Riya gasps and I can practically see new moisture between her toned thighs.

"What do you think, beautiful?" I ask her, pressing one finger against her clit. "Fifteen nice hard strokes so you don't forget your masters?"

"I don't... ow!" She squeals, because I don't wait for a reply. A perfect red line appears just under the first. "*Veck*, Riya," I curse. "You look good with my marks." I bring the crop down again and again, enjoying the swish and crack and the way she moans and writhes at each strike. By the time I'm done, she's kicking up her heels and yelping, and neither of us can wait much longer for release.

I toss the crop aside and run both palms over her heated ass, rubbing and stroking, because I know this turns her pain to pleasure and makes her even needier for my cock. Sure enough, she pushes back into me with her body, hard, forcing her firm ass cheeks into my hands, and begs, "Please, *veck* me, Jax."

I'm already there, and as I push against her soft folds, she shifts her stance to accommodate me, going up on tiptoe and tilting her hips upward.

No matter how wet she gets, her sweet cunt is so *vecking* tight, and I have to go slowly at first, easing into her body.

"Riya," I mutter. Today she feels better than ever—how is it possible that each time is so good?

"Jax," she moans, and the sound of my name on her lips inflames me. I start to thrust, harder and harder, and she matches my moves like she did for Ronan, bracing on the hoverdisk and pushing back into me to maximize our pleasure. Taking her from behind is one of my favorite ways because it allows me to get so *veck*ing deep into her body, and it's only seconds before I'm ready to come. I know she's more than ready by the way she's gasping and pleading with me for release.

"Come, Riya," I snap, and she cries out, unintelligible sounds of passion as we both explode, my pleasure bursting like fire throughout my body. Her orgasm goes on and on, even after I finish, as she continues to clench her pussy and twist her hips, wringing every burst of pleasure she can from my cock. Finally, she sinks forward onto the hoverdisk and gasps, panting.

I ease out of her and scoop her up, then lie her down on the hoverdisk so I can hold her and relax. As my heartrate comes back to normal, I can feel hers still pounding, and I smile, touching the drops of sweat at her brow. *Veck*, it feels good to make her come apart with such pleasure.

Ronan comes up with her fleece and places it over her, then lies beside her, stroking her shoulder. Tarren sits on the edge of the hoverdisk to run his fingers along her calf. And as I lie holding her, my cousins all around us, I feel that life is perfect at this moment. Our family and Zandia are safe and growing. The future is bright.

EPILOGUE

Riya

"What did you name them?" Lily asks.

"What?" I am so mesmerized with their small perfect faces, their tiny little fingers, that I don't even pay attention.

The smaller baby fusses a little bit, and I stroke him, murmuring soothing words, and he settles down with a little gasp, the petal of his mouth opens like a flower, his lids fluttering, his lashes already impossibly long. He has a little dark fuzz on his head, the color of mine, and the most adorable tiny horns.

His brother is larger and louder. When he cries, he wails like the planet is dying, but when he sleeps, he falls so deeply into his slumber that a storm could crash through the room and he wouldn't awaken. Right now, his hands are clenched into fists and he breathes in deeply. I wonder what he's dreaming.

"Their names?" Lily sits beside me on the hoverdisk. "Have you decided?"

"We picked Tarrian for the big one, because he's so like his father. And Ronan's son is Rylan."

"Tarrian and Rylan. Sweet babies. I love their names." She squeezes my hand. "Nice work, Mama. They're perfect."

I wiggle and preen, even though it was out of my control. "I love them," I say simply.

"How is Jax taking it?" She pauses and lowers her voice. "I don't mean to imply that he should have an issue, or that he does. But... does he? I could see how some Zandians, maybe, might?" She bites her lip.

"He's fine." He really is. "He's so laid back nothing seems to bother him. He said that all it means is that he needs to *veck* me a lot more in the future." I blush, but she smiles.

"Also," I disclose, "Dr. Daneth gave me the tools to monitor my ovulation exactly with the thermo-monitor and scanner. It will tell me exactly when my egg releases, so Jax and I can try on those planet rotations. So we can be sure the next will be his."

"Yes, he's distributing that to all the humans now. He said he's disappointed he didn't have it ready in time for the early teams." Lily smiles. "I have one, since we're trying now." She bounces a little. "I think I want to have twins, too."

"I think it's going to be a lot of work." I look at the babies. They're quiet now, but when they're awake and both want to nurse? Mother Earth, it's impossible to fill them fast enough! Also, the crying is enough to shatter eardrums of steel. Tarrian is... loud. Very loud. I smile indulgently. I can't wait to see my boys grow... learn to talk and walk. I already love them so fiercely.

"Your mates will help," she assures me. "And so will your

friends. Lamira asked me to set up a visit/share program for new mothers, to ensure they are getting support and not falling into postpartum depression."

"It's a good idea," I agree. How far we've come since those early planet rotations—not all that long ago—when I first entered my dome, nervous, asking when I'd even get to see my friends again. Now I have mates, and babies, and an entire community. It's miraculous.

My mates enter the chamber, all of them, just as Rylan wakes up and begins to scream. He may not be as loud as his brother, but he's very persistent, and his little face reddens as he shrieks.

Ronan doesn't miss a beat. He scoops up the infant and soothes him, patting his back, until the baby hiccups and settles down. "Want me to change him?" he asks. Without waiting for an answer, he heads to the little station we've set up with diapers and supplies and gets to work.

"I should go," Lily says, and bends to give me a hug. "I'll visit again soon. I love you."

"You too." I smile as she leaves, and then turn my attention to my men—all five of them.

Tarren sits beside me and kisses me. "Dr. Daneth said you can start walking more this planet rotation, if you'd like." I had a surgical birth, because the twins came early. Dr. Daneth cut open my belly to get the babies out. But everything is fine now.

"The big question," says Ronan, looking up from Rylan's diaper, "is when you can start *vecking*. Did he tell us that?"

"He said a few weeks." I laugh. "Until then, make your palm your friend, my love."

Ronan lifts his son's small hand and taps his palm to the tiny one. "Little man, your mother says I have to make do with my hand. Commiserate with me, son. And learn well, how your own palm will become your friend someday."

"Stop! That's disgusting! You can't talk to a baby like that!" But I'm laughing.

"What? My son needs to learn compassion, as well as self-care, and he should start now. Don't worry. He can't understand me yet."

"He can understand everything you say," I argue. "My babies are geniuses."

"Then they will understand how hard this is on their fathers." He rolls his eyes.

"I'm interested in the few weeks' timeframe," Jax says, giving me a kiss. "Because I plan to put another one of these in your belly as soon as possible."

I smile. The thought of his child makes my heart melt. "He'll be gorgeous, like you." I touch his face.

"I have a feeling we'll have a daughter," Jax says. "And she'll be beautiful like you." He turns to the others. "And she'll probably have her brothers, and all of us, wrapped around her tiny fingers."

I can already see her, this vision of a small girl, and I tear up. "I hope so, Jax."

Tarren picks up Tarrian. The sturdy little baby doesn't even stir, but when Tarren holds him against his chest, the child sighs and snuggles in, as if recognizing his father's touch and scent. Who knows—maybe he does. We have much to learn about babies who are half Zandian, half human. We don't truly understand which traits they will inherit from humans.

As my mates gather around me, holding our young, I'm filled with peace and joy.

"I never dared dream I'd have this—any of this," I say.

"Freedom from slavery. One mate, much less three. Babies."
My eyes swim with tears. "And now I have it all."

My mates tighten their circle around me, stroking my
hair back from my face, kissing the top of my head.

"We dreamed. We dreamed of winning back Zandia.
Being near our crystals again." Jax strokes a thumb down my
cheek and I lean into his palm. "But we had no idea the real
treasure on Zandia would be you."

"That's right," Tarren agrees.

"What he said." Ronan flashes his boyish grin.

I blink back the tears and smile up at them, my heart full
to bursting. "I love you."

And then they smother me with kisses, making me
giggle, the moment complete.

***

Thank you for reading *Night of the Zandians*! If you
enjoyed it, we would really appreciate it if you would leave a
review. Your reviews are invaluable to indie authors in
marketing books.

WANT MORE?

Night of the Zandians Bonus Scenes!

Click here to read the scenes where Tarren and Riya first meet, and one with Riya reflecting on what happened with the Ocretion guards.

Please enjoy this excerpt from *Bought by the Zandians*, Zandian Brides Book 2, coming soon!

Bought by the Zandians - Chapter One
Aurelia Minor 2, Slave Auction

Danica

Naked, strapped to a post on the auction block, I suck the blood from my cracked lower lip.

Please let this be quick.

The longer I stand up here, trembling and on full display, the greater the chance of some being searching my barcode and discovering me wanted.

I guarantee my former master, Akron, put a bounty on

my head the moment he realized I escaped. And he doesn't even know the secret I'm keeping. The one that would spell my death.

Yeah.

So it was escape or die. And I escaped. Briefly.

Three Ocretions walk by chortling to themselves. One of them slaps my tit and the three of them roar with laughter. I make my stare blank, like no sentient being is inside my body, as I fiercely pray they won't stop. Ocretions would know to check my slave barcode and trace my history back to Akron. It wouldn't take them more than half a planet rotation to find out about the bounty and deliver me to my rightful owner.

I hold my breath until they move on.

Other than them, I really don't care who buys me. I plan to escape again as soon as possible. Supposedly, there's a planet where human slaves can go and be free. Jesel. It's wildly dangerous, but that doesn't bother me. My life is probably forfeit, anyway.

I wriggle in my tight straps. The animal hide bites into my skin. My arms and legs have gone numb, but worst of all, the one around my neck is too tight and I can scarcely breathe. I work to slow my inhalations, because panic will only make this worse.

The market is full of beings of every species. Most appear too poor to even offer twenty steins for me.

Of course, I don't look like much. I'm filthy and bruised, covered in scrapes from getting here. When I first arrived, I rubbed some of the crimson dirt from this planet on my hair to cover the exotic color. Blondes are considered a rarity amongst human slaves. Unfortunately, I was caught moments later. At least I was grabbed by a small-minded, greedy smuggler, whose only interest was a quick sale.

Two large purple beings with horns stroll idly along the stalls of the market. Muscles bulge beneath their clean white tunics and they carry old-fashioned swords on their belts.

Real Zandian warriors.

I've never seen one before, but I've heard of them. They study for battle until it becomes an art. Long rumored to be extinct, the recent word around the galaxy is they just took back their planet with a tiny army.

They look at me from across the crimson dirt expanse and one of them leans into the other one and says something. When they start walking toward me, my heart inexplicably hammers.

I moisten my cracked lips with my tongue. I can't decide if my response means I'm afraid or excited.

Afraid. Definitely afraid. Warriors like these are probably bounty hunters. They're after the price on my head.

And that may be true, but as they come closer, tingles run across my skin. Must be the damn breeding hormones. I'm never excited by males.

But maybe I just hadn't met the right species before. Because when they stop in front of me, my nipples tighten, breath shortens. Apparently purple aliens with horns are exactly my type.

One of them inhales deeply, his nostrils flaring.

The other one reaches out and slides his thick fingers under the animal hide strap that binds my neck to the post. My eyes fly wide and I try to suck in a breath against the increased constriction. But then he yanks it away from me, tearing it from the post and throwing it to the ground. I drag in a lungful of air and cough.

The Aurelian trader lifts the same gun he used on me

and points it at the male's chest. "Get back! You can't set her free."

Neither Zandian moves. They don't flinch at the sight of the gun, nor do they lift their hands in surrender. "Your slave was choking," my liberator says mildly. He has a deep voice that does strange things to my knees. "You should take care with how tight you strap them. No one will buy a dead female."

The trader scoffs and pinches my cheeks, drawing my bleeding lips together. "This one wouldn't die so easily." He shows them the bite mark I left on his arm. "She's a *liineor*."

I have no idea what a *liineor* is, but I assume it's some wild beast from this planet.

The Zandians don't move, but the upper lip on the leaner one starts to curl. He says something under his breath in their language, and his friend nods. Neither of them have taken their gazes from me.

At first glance, I thought their eyes were brown, but now I see they're purple, like their skin. Or have they grown *more* violet? The leaner one takes a long, slow perusal of my body. "How much?" He sounds only half interested, but that could be part of the bargaining game.

I can't decide if I *want* their interest. I shouldn't. These males are dangerous. Very dangerous. They're trained to kill, and they appear highly intelligent.

So I should be hoping they mosey away and find some other vendor to hassle.

But instead I find myself praying they buy me. For no reason other than that I can't stand the thought of them walking away.

The larger one lifts my tangled hair from my shoulders and peers at my neck. His fingers brush my bare shoulder. He's so close I smell the scent of his skin—masculine and clean. He drops the locks back in place and says something to his friend in Zandian.

Fuck.

They *are* smart. He just saw my real hair color but he's playing it cool.

"Where did you get her?" he asks. He has a square, hairless jaw and a cleft chin that probably makes every female in the galaxy drool when he goes by.

The trader lifts his chin. "It doesn't matter where."

"So you don't have her file? She's not legally yours?" the leaner one asks.

Oh fuck. They're asking way too many questions. The next thing you know, they'll be checking my barcode. I twist my neck to the side and lean forward, catching the "V" of skin showing above the Zandian's tunic with my tongue. I flick once. Twice.

He catches me by the hair and pulls my head back, gazing down at me with amusement.

"I think she likes you," his friend observes with a chuckle.

He's holding my hair in a fist too tight, but I don't think he means to hurt me. He's just too strong, or unaware how much weaker my species is. He leans down and brushes his lips across mine. At the same time, his free hand cups my mons.

I jerk, more from surprise, than anything. And because every other time a male has grabbed me there has been unpleasant.

But it isn't this time. He rubs the pad of his finger lightly through my folds and I'm stunned at how wet I am.

His horns stiffen and lean in my direction while he watches my face, his nose almost touching mine, amethyst eyes burning.

I pant, heat curling like smoke through my belly.

"One hundred fifty stein," he says. He removes his finger from my pussy. I'm itchy and hot. Needy for his touch to return.

"Three hundred," the vendor counters.

"One seventy-five. Final offer." He releases my hair and takes a step back.

"Two fifty."

His friend scoffs. He shrugs and walks away.

The fucking vendor lets them go. Three steps away. Four. Five. "Two hundred," he calls to their backs.

They stop but don't turn. They seem to be in conversation with each other.

"One ninety."

It takes the broad one two long strides to return. His friend pulls out a burlap bag full of coins while he digs his fingers under the strap around my chest. He rips it off, as if thick animal hide is easy to snap.

I wince as the blood rushes down my arms like a million insect stings. He rips off the strap around my thighs and I crumple, unable to hold myself up. In a flash, I'm swooped up over a broad shoulder.

The Zandian claps a large hand down on my ass. "Come on, little slave. We know just the place for humans who like to escape their masters."

Want More? Check out the next books in the Zandian Brides series, *Bought by the Zandians.*

THEY BOUGHT ME AT AUCTION--CLAIMED ME AS THEIRS.

Two purple, horned males with massive chests and arms as thick as my waist.

They're taking me to Zandia to bear their young.

The only trouble--I'm already pregnant.

And if my former master finds me, he'll tear me to pieces once his young is born.

My new masters are firm, but kind. They give far more pleasure than pain. Their planet is beautiful.

But when they find out my secret, I have no doubt they'll cast me out.

And my life will be forfeit.

Because no human female with a bounty on her head survives a lunar cycle alone.

READ NOW

WANT FREE BOOKS?

Go to http://subscribepage.com/alphastemp to sign up for Renee Rose's newsletter and receive a free books. In addition to the free stories, you will also get special pricing, exclusive previews and news of new releases.

OTHER TITLES BY RENEE ROSE

Scoring with Santa

Saved

Other Contemporary

Black Light: Valentine Roulette

Black Light: Roulette Redux

Black Light: Celebrity Roulette

Black Light: Roulette War

Black Light: Roulette Rematch

Punishing Portia (written as Darling Adams)

The Professor's Girl

Safe in his Arms

Paranormal

Bad Boy Alphas Series

Alpha's Temptation

Alpha's Danger

Alpha's Prize

Alpha's Challenge

Alpha's Obsession

Alpha's Desire

Alpha's War

Alpha's Mission

Alpha's Bane

Alpha's Secret

Alpha's Prey

Alpha's Sun

Shifter Ops

Alpha's Moon

Alpha's Vow

Alpha's Revenge

Alpha's Fire

Alpha's Rescue

Alpha's Command

Wolf Ranch Series

Rough

Wild

Feral

Savage

Fierce

Ruthless

Two Marks Series

Untamed

Tempted

Desired

Enticed

Wolf Ridge High Series

Alpha Bully

Alpha Knight

Step Alpha

Midnight Doms

Alpha's Blood

His Captive Mortal

All Souls Night

Alpha Doms Series

The Alpha's Hunger

The Alpha's Promise

The Alpha's Punishment

Other Paranormal

The Winter Storm: An Ever After Chronicle

Sci-Fi

Zandian Masters Series

His Human Slave

His Human Prisoner

Training His Human

His Human Rebel

His Human Vessel

His Mate and Master

Zandian Pet

Their Zandian Mate

His Human Possession

Zandian Brides

Night of the Zandians

Bought by the Zandians

Mastered by the Zandians

Zandian Lights

Kept by the Zandian

ALSO BY REBEL WEST / ALEXIS ALVAREZ

Read More by Rebel West / Alexis Alvarez

Zandian Brides Series (with co-writer Renee Rose)

Night of the Zandians

Bought by the Zandians

Mastered by the Zandians

Zandian Lights

Kept by the Zandian

Claimed by the Zandian

Stolen by the Zandian

Sci-Fi Romance

Conquered by the Alien Prince: Luminar Masters, Book 1

Steamy, Contemporary Romance

Perfect Match

A Handful of Fire

Boston

Dream Girl

Kinky/BDSM Romance

His Firm Direction

Casey's Choice

Capturing Kate

Myka and the Millionaire

Return

ABOUT RENEE ROSE

USA TODAY BESTSELLING AUTHOR RENEE ROSE loves a dominant, dirty-talking alpha hero! She's sold over a half million copies of steamy romance with varying levels of kink. Her books have been featured in USA Today's *Happily Ever After* and *Popsugar*. Named Eroticon USA's Next Top Erotic Author in 2013, she has also won *Spunky and Sassy's* Favorite Sci-Fi and Anthology author, and *The Romance Reviews* Best Historical Romance. She's hit the *USA Today* list seven times with her Wolf Ranch books and various anthologies.

Please follow her on:
  Bookbub | Goodreads | Instagram

Renee loves to connect with readers!
www.reneeroseromance.com
reneeroseauthor@gmail.com

ABOUT REBEL WEST

Rebel West writes hot sci-fi with aliens so sexy you'll swoon! She's into photography and travel, and when she's not figuring out ways to get her main characters together, she's out with her camera looking for inspiration. Find her under her other pen name, Alexis Alvarez, where she writes contemporary romance and kinky/spanky/BDSM books.

Read More by Rebel West / Alexis Alvarez

Sci-Fi Romance
Conquered by the Alien Prince: Luminar Masters, Book 1

Steamy, Contemporary Romance:
Perfect Match
A Handful of Fire
Boston
Dream Girl

Kinky/BDSM Romance:

His Firm Direction
Casey's Choice
Capturing Kate
Myka and the Millionaire
Return

Newsletter: https://goo.gl/forms/iVRhZbk2s0mz8v6h2

Website: http://graffitifiction.com/

Amazon Author Page: https://www.amazon.com/Alexis-Alvarez/e/B0107LJQEM

Facebook Author Page: https://www.facebook.com/AlexisAlvarezAuthor/

Goodreads: https://www.goodreads.com/author/show/14127116.Alexis_Alvarez

Twitter: https://twitter.com/AlexisAlvarezWr

Instagram: https://www.instagram.com/alexis_alvarez_writer/

CONQUERED BY THE ALIEN PRINCE - SAMPLE

Conquered by the Alien Prince
Luminar Masters, Book 1
An Alien Sci-Fi Romance
By Rebel West

A sexy silver alien with ripped abs, a top-secret patient with a mystery illness, and unicorns – and Dr. Emily Taylor's experience on Luminar is just getting started!

It's not easy being one of Earth's top neuroscientists at age twenty-four, but Emily's dedicated her life to research, leaving little time for dating. When she travels on a confidential mission to Luminar, her local delegation lead – handsome Prince Lock, turns out to be domineering in all the right ways to bring out her passion.

But he's an alien prince and she's an earth human, and there's no way they could have a *real* relationship. Plus, anti-human protestors and threats against the Luminar monarchy are causing havoc, putting her mission, and maybe even her life, into jeopardy.

This interplanetary romance will need to have a bond of

steel, because the glorious nights of kinky passion are just the start to an everlasting HEA.

Enjoy the first book in the Luminar Masters Series by Rebel West. The books are interconnected and can be read in any order. Guaranteed HEA and no cheating!

Note: This book contains elements of dominance and submission. If this material offends you, please do not buy this book.

CONQUERED BY THE ALIEN PRINCE - CHAPTER ONE

He was, without question, the sexiest man she'd ever seen.

Well over six feet tall, he was muscular, with a strong chest, ripped abs, and broad shoulders. Dark hair, large eyes and eyelashes, chiseled cheekbones, and lush lips. The way his pants rode low on his hips? She wanted to lick his muscular ridges.

Yes, he was clearly the sexiest man alive. Except he wasn't, technically, a *man* at all. He was an alien, a silvery, shimmery prince from the planet Luminar. His hair was a deep midnight blue, as were his eyes. And as he spoke on the holo vid, it was like he was looking straight into her soul.

Emily shifted on the bed, ignoring the tinge of arousal that sparked through her body. Even if she was headed to Luminar as a scientific delegate, she wouldn't interact with royalty– and she had better things to do than lust over a complete stranger from another planet.

Still, she leaned forward, fascinated, as he spoke. "... grateful that our two worlds have come together to create a permanent IRT, or Interplanetary Research Team. As a part of this new endeavor, we will allow human and Luminarian scientists to visit each other's planet under local guidance and supervision..." The prince was fluent in English, and he spoke with a faint accent that sounded almost European.

Behind him, a crowd surged, cheering, lots of silvery aliens. Evident as well were the protestors, an angry mob of dissenters, whose chant grew louder as they approached the area.

"No humans no more!" flashed on screen, a translation for the alien tongue. *"Humans not welcome! Never again!"*

"And we'll be back after this message," said the Earth broadcaster smoothly, as the holo vid from Luminar cut to an ad. Emily frowned, wishing to see more of the prince...and his bare chest. It was fascinating that Luminarian males often went around without shirts.

"Emily?"

Her interest in the program lost since the alien planet had been replaced with some local human-interest story, Emily turned her head. "Yes?"

"Dinner's ready! Come on out, 'kay?"

"I will! I was just watching about the Luminarians and the IRT. They showed that hot prince who's been the spokesperson for their government...and protesters. Also, packing." She patted the small pile of things on her bed.

Maya appeared in the doorway. "The right wingers are protesting here on Earth, too, every time a group of Luminarian delegates arrive."

Emily snorted, feeling the usual chest tightness that came from thinking about all of Earth's turmoil.

Maya added, "They say that they're worried that the aliens really want to steal our tech and learn about our world so they can take it from us. Kill us all, or something. Maybe engineer a super virus to take us all out."

"It's a legit concern, even if they're overdramatizing it."

Emily leaned forward. "Any time two new worlds collide, even if they're friendly..." She shook her head. "I've never gotten the impression that the Luminarians have nefarious intentions, but, I mean, I'm not the expert on the depths of alien psychology and strategy." *His eyes, though – no being with that kind of gaze, that fervent sincerity to his voice, could be dangerous. Right?*

"At least President Matumba, and the Luminar leaders, have made it clear that they want to work together peacefully. So there's that." Maya sighed.

"Right? Plus, by all accounts, Luminar has the more advanced tech compared to us. I'm not sure there's much we have that they need to steal." Emily raised an eyebrow. "Although we're ahead of them in atmospheric science and carbon dioxide control."

Maya sat down on the bed. "The fringe protesters here want our government to wipe out their planet. Or they say we need to engineer a super virus ourselves just in case we need it to destroy them."

"And knowing our government...we probably already are working on a virus." Emily lowered her voice. "Look what they've done right at home."

She gestured around the room, but both women knew she wasn't referring to her bedroom or the apartment they shared, but to *The Villages* - desolate patches of wasteland, full of angry gangs and dead land. To the city they lived in, full of high tech and coffee shops and trees, places where you could buy caviar with gold flakes, and also to the swathes of bleakness caused by war and civil unrest. "Parts of the Northern United America are like patches of third world now. It's insane."

"Luminar and Earth have similar atmospheres. We could survive on their planet and they could survive here."

Maya wrapped her arms around herself. "I hope the delegations make sure we get along, you know? And truly help each other."

Emily nodded. "Maybe they'll actually be interested in proliferating things like *Inculon*." Tears came to her eyes and she swiped them away hard.

"I hate that." Maya grabbed Em's hand. "You worked for so many years on that, Em. You gave up your life to make that drug and do the testing."

"It still makes me insane if I think about it." Emily's voice trembled. "Do you know how cheaply it can be made? Pennies. And they sell it for thousands of dollars and people are dying in the Villages because they can't afford it. And it's my fault."

"Em, they stole the patent from you."

"It was all legal." Emily shook her head. "And I was stupid. Because I developed the drug while I was working for InGen, they have the rights. And sell it they do. For an insane profit. They'll strip my medical license if I do anything with it."

"That's so fucking unfair." Maya scowled.

"Yeah. It is. But I'm smarter now, which is why I teach and work at the non-profit. And I know that someday I'll make something even better, and this time it won't be stolen by greedy industry thugs." Emily's voice gained strength. "I know it."

"You will." Maya squeezed Em. "You're brilliant. I have no doubts."

"Thank you." Emily hugged back. "You're so nice to me."

Maya smiled. "The aliens will be nice to you, too. I promise."

Em laughed. "We'll see."

"It's crazy that we've only known about them for twenty

years, but they've known about us for centuries." Maya's voice got softer. "Do you think all those alien sightings over the years were them, watching us? *Stealing* us for research?"

Emily shook her head. "I have no idea. They certainly don't look like the aliens anyone ever drew." She smiled at her friend. "But look at those guys, right? I bet more people - - women, anyway, would be lining up to be *abducted*," she made air quotes on the word, "If they knew aliens were so sexy."

Maya laughed. "You're so going to end up in bed with one of them. I can see it now." She waved her hand and deepened her voice. "Earth human -- is that what they call us?" She stood up and broadened her stance. "Earth human and renowned neurologist, gorgeous twenty-four year old Doctor Emily Taylor, breaks her three year dry spell by fucking -- do they say that? A super-hot silver alien from Luminar. I'm reporting from her bedroom, where she's currently licking --"

"Stop!" Emily tossed a pair of balled up socks at her friend. "You're disgusting."

"Oh, really? Please. I see the pictures of those aliens on the news, and there is not an unattractive one in the bunch. Compare that to the Earth politicians and scientists that they're going to meet. I feel sorry for them." She laughed. "President Matumba is fierce, but that gut? And think about the disgusting, flabby senators on CSPAX. And didn't you tell me that your lab assistant Gary likes to actually sit there and pop his pimples while he's waiting for experiments to run?"

"Uh, yes. Yes, I did. Now I'm not hungry for dinner, thank you very much." Emily rolled her eyes. "Because he wipes the pus on his pants that he never washes!"

The two women collapsed together, screaming in

disgust. "Alien women will not want to go near him," said Maya.

"Nobody wants to go near him," Emily said, shaking her head. "But I'm not going there to meet someone. I'm focused on work, you know that."

"I thought those undercover investigation reports said that there actually have been secret intermarriages and relationships, lots of them, between Luminarians and humans over the past twenty years," Maya said, her face lighting up. "The babies they showed on *World Enquirer's* vid channel were adorable."

"Photoshopped. And I'm going for research." Emily raised a hand to stop Maya's next comment before she uttered it. "*Just* for research."

Maya wasn't deterred. "So you say. But since it's top secret, and you refuse to tell me the details, I'm just going to have to assume it's really a mail-order bride deal, and you'll come home with a pocket full of cute silver babies."

"It's a confidential government project. I can't tell you, or I'd have to kill you." Emily laughed. The truth was that even she didn't know what her project really was, yet -- not entirely.

The invitation to visit had come in an encrypted tele-disc from the government office of interplanetary research -- a request directly from Luminar for her to visit and consult on a high-level top-secret patient.

She'd said yes, without a second thought. She'd received clearance, and encouragement, from the government and her institute to participate. Now...she was anxiously awaiting her departure, wondering if her decision was the best one she'd ever made...or the most foolish.

"Well, in honor of your departure, and the way I'm going to miss you, I cooked myself. From scratch! Using real food.

Awesome, right? Just in case you starve over the next few months eating their beetles and bark."

"It smells amazing. And I don't think they actually eat insects."

"I just want you to be careful." Maya grabbed Emily's hand and squeezed. "Be safe there. I don't like those crowds of anti-human protesters." Her brow wrinkled. "Seriously."

"I don't like them, either." Emily bit her lip, nerves jangling. Yet how could she give up the chance to visit another planet? Who got that chance in their lifetime?

She'd never believed in destiny, but from the second she'd heard about Luminar and the fact that scientists would be allowed to participate in joint research, her entire body longed to go there, like it was the only thing that mattered anymore. She couldn't wait.

Read Conquered by the Alien Prince

www.ingramcontent.com/pod-product-compliance
Lightning Source LLC
Chambersburg PA
CBHW020618110726
47899CB00002B/552